Saltwater

Orchard

A Haven Collection Story

Evelyn Grace

Three Strands Publishing, LLC

Contents

He has told you, O man, what is good;
and what does the Lord require of you
but to do justice,
and to love kindness,
and to walk humbly with your God?
Micah 6:8

One

R yann Jordan knew she should have stayed in bed today.

The clocks changed yesterday. She was now sleep deprived and dreading the mud that always plagued Maine this time of year. But that was the least of her worries.

She grabbed the coffee cup as it started sliding off the end of her tray, catching it before it slammed to the floor. Ryann saved the mug from breaking, but coffee dripped down the front of her shirt and apron, pooling on the floor at her feet. Just great.

Her day began with her landlord banging on her door an hour before her alarm went off. And the day had continued going downhill from there.

Colleen, one of the three sisters who owned the Three Cat Café, gently nudged Ryann toward the back. "It's just coffee. I have a spare shirt and apron out back. Why don't you go change? I'll clean this up."

Ryann blew a puff of air out, fluffing her bangs up, as she started towards the back offices. "Lord, I could use a little help today," she whispered under her breath as she went to change.

Her mind was going in too many directions. She was having a hard time focusing on what she needed to do right now because she kept thinking about what she'd need to do tonight. Move.

She hadn't planned on moving, but ever since Stan, her landlord, had shown up this morning, she knew she needed to leave as soon as possible. She couldn't remember everything he'd said, and he'd left before she could do more than rub the sleep out of her eyes.

The only reason Ryann could think of for his actions was the fact that she'd rebuffed his advances more than once. He seemed to think since she had a daughter and no ring on her finger, it meant she would sleep with anyone. Stan didn't realize her daughter once had a father, or that Ryann had been married. It wasn't something she talked much about with anyone. And it certainly wasn't a conversation she would have with someone like Stan.

It probably didn't help that she'd also made more than one complaint to the town about how he ran the trailer park. Getting Stan to fix anything took multiple complaints and often threats. Rats had come around the piled-up garbage, which he never seemed to have time to clean up. That's when she'd had enough. She'd called the town to file a formal complaint. Stan had been furious about the fine he'd gotten.

Stan had told her this morning she had twenty-four hours to get out or else. She didn't know what he meant by "or else", but she wouldn't stick around to find out either. Ryann no longer had the energy to fight with Stan. And she wouldn't keep looking over her shoulder, watching for him to show up to harass her. She would pack what she could carry and leave the rest without looking back. Where she would go, she didn't know, but it had to be better than dealing with Stan.

Walking into Colleen's office, she found the spare apron and shirt hanging on a peg just inside the door. Ryann exchanged her wet top for the dry one and tied the clean apron around her waist. She hurried to transfer her pens, receipts, and tips from the wet apron to the one she was now wearing. She bundled the wet clothing into a plastic bag to bring home.

"Lord, I'm not sure what you want me to learn from all of this, but please give me clarity." The only thing that had ever helped her get through life had been her relationship with God.

She continued to think of all the potential places to go tonight. Ryann had told no one at work about her need to move. She knew the sisters who owned the café would help her if she only asked. She'd seen Colleen, Abigail, and Brenda do it before, for others. There wasn't much that went on in this town that they didn't know about.

Haven was one of those small towns where everyone knew everyone else. It was the reason Ryann had always planned to leave as soon as possible. She wanted to start a life where she wasn't defined by her parents or where she lived.

Her goal had once included plans to attend Bowdoin College to study biology. It was one of the top science schools in Maine. She'd dreamed of going since she was nine years old and had seen an ad for the college while her dad was watching a TV show.

Ryann still remembered how her father had laughed when she said she was going to go there someday. "We can't pay for you to go to some fancy pants college, kiddo. Better get that out of your head right now."

Her father had been right. There was no way her parents could help with the tuition, especially not when the paper mill closed. Her father had drifted from one dead-end job to another after that. They'd barely had enough money to pay their bills, let alone contribute to college costs.

Ryann had worked long and hard, saving every penny she made and working to get the best grades she could. When her acceptance letter had come in, she'd been so happy. She couldn't wait to work towards her goal, but life had other plans.

If Ryann had made her dream come true, she would be a biologist now. She'd be working in a lab, helping to find cures to diseases. Diseases like the one her little girl was now facing.

Shaking off the memories of a past she couldn't change, she turned to go check on her daughter. Erica was playing down the hall in Brenda's office. Their regular sitter had canceled at the last minute. Since her seven-year-old daughter couldn't stay by herself, she'd brought her to work with her.

Ryann suspected the sitter had canceled because she still didn't feel comfortable watching Erica since her new diagnosis, even after all these weeks. Ryann couldn't blame the woman. There was a lot to consider when caring for Erica these days.

Ryann sighed. It was one more thing to deal with. While the sisters were great about allowing her to bring Erica to the café when she needed to, she knew it wasn't fair to any of them to have the little girl there all the time. She needed to find a new sitter.

Ryann slowed as she approached the office door. Her daughter's voice floated out to her.

"Now, this won't hurt a bit. We're just going to check your blood sugar. Here, give me your finger. Okay, one, two, three. ..just a little pinch. There now. That wasn't so bad, was it?"

Pushing the door open a crack, Ryann peeked inside to see Erica on the floor with her teddy bear and blood sugar testing supplies. Ryann covered her mouth, swallowing hard as she worked to hold back the tears.

Even after a month, it was difficult to accept that Erica had been diagnosed with Type 1 diabetes and would now need to check her blood sugar levels and receive multiple injections every day to survive. Why couldn't life be fair?

At least Erica was getting the hang of testing her own blood sugars and helping with her shots. Ryann sometimes couldn't believe just how strong her little girl was in the face of all these changes.

Ryann pushed the door the rest of the way open and stepped through. "Hey, sweetie. You okay?"

"Hi, Mommy!"

It hadn't taken long for Erica to tell her mother how much she disliked being asked what her blood sugar was all the time. Ryann was still working on not hovering over her daughter constantly.

She'd also learned just how expensive this disease could be. So far, her insurance was still denying the request for a continuous glucose monitor and an insulin pump. The technology would have eliminated the need for multiple finger sticks or shots every day. It would have allowed Ryann to track Erica's blood sugars right on her phone. That peace of mind would have been wonderful to have. However, the insurance company wanted them to work with injections for a few more months before they would even consider paying for any of the equipment.

"I'm just checking Mr. Bear's blood sugar. It's a little low. I think he needs a cookie."

"He does, does he? Can I double check?" She took a seat on the floor beside her daughter and waited for permission.

"Sure."

Ryann picked up the testing kit. Thirty days ago, she hadn't known what diabetes entailed. She hadn't known what a normal blood sugar was or even how to test to see if it fell in the correct range. Now she thought she could do a finger stick with her eyes closed.

After pretending to check the teddy bear's blood sugar, Ryann reached for her daughter's finger. "Your turn." Erica made a face, but let Ryann draw the bead of blood needed. They both watched the five second countdown. The number appeared. 65.

"Well, it looks like Mr. Bear needs a cookie after all. Let's go see what Brenda has in the kitchen."

"Yeah!" Erica jumped to her feet, eager not only for the sweet treat, but to see Brenda as well. Her daughter enjoyed spending time in the kitchen with Brenda. And she always made time for Erica also.

Ryann took her daughter's hand and headed to the kitchen. She needed to get back to her tables, but this came first. Erica often dropped fast once her blood sugar started going low.

"Well, look who it is! My favorite little seven-year-old." Brenda smiled as Erica and Ryann walked through the door. She ruled the kitchen at the Three Cats and was a whiz with all things sweet. "Looking for a snack?"

Erica nodded her head. "Yes, please!"

"Well, I have some chocolate chip cookies hot out of the oven that are about as big as your head! How about one of those with a nice glass of milk?" Brenda looked at Ryann for confirmation. Everyone at the café had been wonderful in supporting Ryann and Erica through this new phase of life.

"Half a cookie and the milk will be more than enough," Ryann said. She would need to give Erica some insulin to cover the sugar in the snack. There was more sugar between the cookie and the milk than was needed to bring her daughter's blood sugar back to a normal range. Otherwise, they would deal with a rebound high in a few hours.

Erica's smile slid off her face, but quickly came back as Brenda broke a cookie in half, plated it, and poured a small glass of milk. Brenda hadn't been wrong about the size of the cookie. Even though it was only half, it almost filled the small plate.

"Table three is looking for you. Leave her here with me while you take care of that and bring table five their orders. Things are slowing down." Brenda reached out and patted Ryann's shoulder.

"I need to give her a shot."

"Mommy, you can give it to me in a couple of minutes."

Ryann contemplated all the variables it took these days to balance her daughter's blood sugar with Erica's need to live a normal life. Nodding to herself, she replied, "Alright, sweetie. I'll be right back. But count to thirty–slowly–before you eat the cookie, okay? But you can start on the milk."

"Okay." The little girl beamed a smile at Ryann. Grabbing the glass, she took a long swallow of milk. She set it down and gave Ryann another smile, complete with a milk mustache.

Even though Ryann chuckled as she went to grab the food, her heart was heavy. She couldn't forget how close she'd come to losing her daughter when she was diagnosed. Erica's blood sugar had been dangerously high, and she could have slipped into a coma if Ryann had waited a few more minutes.

She gave herself a mental shake. No more what ifs. God had protected her daughter that day and she trusted He would continue to do so.

Ryann mumbled another prayer under her breath as she headed out to the front to check on her customers. "God, give us the strength we need to get through this. Protect my little girl. And please give me wisdom about what to do next."

Two

Richard

R ichard Mosely tried not to drum his fingers on the table. He was having a hard time paying attention. The meeting contributed nothing to his goal of becoming the newest vice president of the bank, and that was where his sole focus was lately. Yet here he was anyway. He worked to get his attention back on the discussion.

He couldn't keep his gaze from flickering towards the window. The spring breeze was blowing the pine trees, causing them to sway. He knew it would be colder out on the ocean, but it was a perfect spring day. A day where he wanted to be on the water up around Haven, where he'd spent his childhood summers.

"Richard, what are your thoughts?"

His mind slammed back to the present as he worked to hide the fact his head had been out tacking sail rather than focused on the meeting. The last thing he needed was for the bank president to catch him daydreaming. Richard rewound the meeting discussion in his head and found the question that had been asked.

"I think we need more information. This seems like a high risk to the bank. Do the financials back up their ability to pay back the loan?"

"That's in table three on page forty-five."

And just like that, the conversation shifted once more. Richard let out the breath he'd been holding as he waited to see if he'd be reprimanded for not paying attention. He made more of an effort to stay engaged as the meeting progressed.

He didn't need Adam Washer to know he'd faltered there for a moment. Not only was Adam the bank president, but he was the father of Richard's girlfriend Sloane.

"Okay, we're adjourned. We'll meet again on Friday to make a final decision. Thank you all." Adam rapped the table with his knuckles twice before standing, like he always did at the end of a meeting.

Richard rose and scurried back to his office before Adam could comment on his lack of engagement during the meeting. He sank behind his desk and opened his email. A smile crossed his face as he reread the one he'd received yesterday afternoon from the vice president of loans.

He would meet with the man that afternoon. The promotion was almost his. Richard's career was heading the way he wanted. Finally.

Banking hadn't been his first choice. While he'd majored in business, he hadn't planned to work at a bank. His goal had always been to start his own company. Be his own boss. He'd taken the bank job to gain work experience, nothing more.

Except life hadn't worked that way. He'd graduated college with a mountain of student loan debt. Central Bank in Portland was the first to offer him a job out of college. He'd started as a teller, working his way up the corporate ladder. And he found he was good at it. He even enjoyed it.

Richard had planned to work at the bank for a few years while paying off his student loans. Except one year turned into two, which turned into five, and now here he was, ten years later, working in the loan office with a promotion just around the corner. He smiled once more at the thought of becoming a vice president in the loan division. He'd been working hard to be noticed, and it was finally paying off.

He felt a slight twinge at the thought of how far he was from the dream of owning his own business. Over the years, Richard had written up several business plans. They'd included everything from a juice bar to a full restaurant to a car rental scheme. All had been good ideas, but none had been *the* idea. The one that would make him get out of bed, eager to go to work daily.

Except if he'd followed any of those dreams, he would have never met Sloane Washer. He smiled as thoughts of his girlfriend filled his mind.

Three years ago, Richard had attended the office Christmas party where he met Sloane for the first time. They'd been dating for two months before Richard had realized Sloane and Adam were related.

It wasn't until he'd received an invitation to a family cookout. He was surprised to find Adam in the kitchen, wearing jeans and a t-shirt and standing barefoot. Richard had never seen

Adam out of a suit before. However, Adam had welcomed him with a firm handshake and assured Richard that their personal relationship wouldn't affect his treatment of Richard at work.

So far, Adam had kept his word. And he certainly hoped Adam would continue to mean it because Richard was planning to propose to Sloane. Tonight.

Richard had picked out the perfect ring. He'd made the reservations months ago. The small, intimate Italian restaurant, Trattoria Ricci in the Old Port, would be perfect.

The buzzing of his office intercom interrupted his musings. He still had a smile on his face when he punched the button to talk to the receptionist. "Yes?"

"There's a courier here with a package. You need to come sign for it."

That was odd. Andrea usually signed for all packages. "You can't do it?"

"Sorry, no. The courier insists he needs you to sign in person."

He could hear the frustration in Andrea's voice. She didn't like being told no by anyone, even if it was just a courier. "Fine. I'll be right there."

Punching the off button, he stood and hurried to the front desk. A messenger was shifting from foot to foot, eager to be on his way.

"Are you Richard Mosely?"

"I am."

"Sign here." The courier thrust a clipboard towards him, pointing to a line.

Richard scribbled his signature and handed the clipboard back.

"Have a nice day." The messenger grabbed the clipboard and shoved a manila envelope at Richard before spinning on his heel and hurrying away.

Richard walked back to his office as he examined the outside of the envelope. A label on the front had his name and work address on it. There was nothing else to give him a clue as to who had sent it.

He dropped into his office chair. Opening the flap, he pulled out a sheaf of papers.

"Well, huh..." His voice trailed off as he took in the words at the top of the page. *The Last Will and Testament of Arnold Carruthers*. His uncle had died. Well, technically, the man had been his great-uncle, his mother's uncle.

Unexpected emotions filled him as Richard read. He hadn't gone to see Uncle Art much in the last few years. And he hadn't even spoken to him on the phone in at least six months. Richard swallowed hard as he continued to read.

A light tap on his door made him look up. "Everything okay?" Andrea entered Richard's office, a folder in her hand.

"Yeah," he cleared his throat and continued, "my great-uncle died. They sent me a copy of his will."

"You didn't know he'd died?" Andrea's eyebrows rose. "I'm sorry."

"Well," Richard rubbed the back of his neck with one hand, "I haven't been great about staying in touch. Still, I'm not sure why no one called me."

Richard cleared his throat again, shoving emotions down. He wasn't about to let anything but his professionalism show at the office.

"Did you need me for something?" He looked up and saw sympathy on Andrea's face. He regretted not talking to his uncle more, but he was busy building a life here in Portland. Uncle Art would have understood that.

"He must have left you something." Andrea walked over to drop the file on his desk. "Adam wants that by two o'clock today."

"Adam left me something?" Richard was confused. What would Adam have left him?

"No, silly. Your uncle. That's the only reason they would have sent you a copy of the will." She turned to leave. "Let me know what you got." She smiled over her shoulder as she walked out the door. "Maybe he left you buried treasure!" She laughed as she continued down the hall.

Richard smiled as his eyes went back to the page. He skimmed through the legalese at the top. Then he stopped, mouth dropping open, as he realized Andrea was right. His uncle had left him something.

I, Arnold Carruthers, a resident of Haven, Maine, being of sound mind, declare this to be my Last Will and Testament. I leave my entire estate comprising my home, barn, and apple orchard and all their contents, in Haven, Maine, to my great-nephew, Richard Mosely, to do with as he wishes once he meets the following stipulation.

He must live on the property and work the land for one year and a day. After that stated time frame, he may sell it, if that is his desire. Richard must take possession of the property within two weeks of receiving notification.

If he refuses this bequest or does not take possession within the stipulated timeframe, he will forfeit the house and land to the Haven Fire Department for whatever purposes they wish to use it for.

Richard stared in disbelief. His uncle had left him the apple farm. He hadn't seen that coming. What was he going to do with a farm?

He continued to read the rest of the will, but the important part was right there at the top. If he were to inherit his uncle's property, he would have to make a drastic life change.

Richard was on the brink of receiving the promotion he'd been working towards for the last year. Now he wasn't sure what to do. Accepting this offer would change everything. He wasn't sure he wanted to become an apple farmer. But now that the offer was in front of him, he wasn't sure he wanted to spend the rest of his life being a banker either.

And what about tonight? Richard couldn't see Sloane moving to Haven and working on a farm. He wasn't sure she even owned a pair of sneakers, let alone work boots. There was no way she'd get her hands dirty and work with him. He tried to picture her digging in the dirt or picking apples and barked out a laugh at just the thought of it.

He sat back in his chair as his mind clouded with indecision. This could derail all his plans. The move would change everything. Yet, he'd always loved the farm. He'd spent nearly every summer at Saltwater Orchard from the time he was around eight years old until he was sixteen.

The summers working beside his uncle in the orchard had been some of his favorites. Taking care of the trees so they would produce fruit in the fall was satisfying work. He remembered with nostalgia how it felt to put in a day of hard work and sleep well, knowing he'd done a good job that day.

Andrea poked her head in the door. "So, what did he leave you? Anything good?"

Richard pulled his attention off the papers and up to the receptionist. "He left me his entire estate. A house, barn, and apple orchard in Haven."

"Woah! Isn't Haven up on the coast somewhere?"

"Yeah, it's a little town near Camden and Rockport."

"What are you going to do with it?"

"I'm not sure. Guess I'll need to figure it out."

Richard stared back down at the will. He analyzed the risk involved. This could be the start of something amazing or it could crash his career. Either way, he had very little time to decide.

Three

Tossing the last article of clothing in the backpack, Ryann zipped it up. She shrugged the bag on even as she looked around to see if she'd missed anything essential. All she really wanted to do was curl up on the couch and watch an episode of *Friends*. But she refused to wait for Stan to come back and bang on her door.

"Erica, hustle up. We need to get moving," Ryann called down the hallway to where she could hear her daughter singing to herself in her bedroom. "Remember, just what you can fit in your backpack."

Ryann went to the kitchen, where she had a duffel bag on the counter. She began packing everything she needed for Erica. Diabetes now meant thinking beyond the moment. It was overwhelming knowing they would be on the move. It made it harder to pack now that she had to think of all the potential scenarios. What if Erica's blood sugar went low or it went high or... she took a deep breath and counted to ten. She'd learned early on that going over every probable scenario just made her anxious.

Taking another deep breath, she continued packing the supplies. She added in the last few juice boxes and a few packages of fruit snacks for emergencies.

"Lord, I don't know what you're trying to teach me, but please help me learn it fast. I don't want to do this. Be with us. Guide us to where we should live. Keep us safe."

Thankfully, Ryann had a full tank of gas. The weather was warming up now that winter was fading. The evenings were still cool, but they could sleep in the car with the heat going if it got too cold at night.

The biggest obstacle would be school. Classes would be out in just a few weeks, though. Ryann would need to talk with Erica about not telling her teacher she was living in a car. That was the last thing she needed anyone knowing.

Homeless. That hadn't been on her radar. No one dreams of being homeless. The plans she'd had for her life had disappeared the moment she'd met Eric. She refused to focus on that now.

Instead, Ryann focused her anger on Stan. She'd been a good tenant. She'd never been late with her rent. Ryann knew she could probably make a stink and stay, but she didn't want to have to deal with Stan anymore. She was done with watching over her shoulder for his next inappropriate comment or sudden appearance. It was time to leave.

"I'm ready, Mommy. Are you sure we can't stay? I'm going to miss my room and my stuffed animals. I'm bringing Mr. Bear with me. Is that okay?"

Ryann turned to her daughter with a quick smile. She was used to the words that Erica shot at her with rapid fire. Her daughter attacked life head on and had done that from the day she was born.

Reaching out, Ryann pushed a strand of dark brown hair behind her little girl's ear. Erica's blue eyes brimmed with unshed tears as she looked for reassurance.

Erica had her daddy's eyes. Ryann allowed herself to think briefly of Eric before she pushed the thought away. There's was a story that didn't have a happy ending, and one she couldn't change. Right now, she needed to focus on a place to live and keeping her daughter healthy.

"You can absolutely bring Mr. Bear with you, sweetie, but we can't stay here. Don't worry. It's going to be an adventure!" Ryann tried to infuse excitement into her voice rather than the worry she was feeling. "We're going to camp out. It'll be fun! Now, let's go load up."

Erica didn't look convinced as she headed out the door, clutching her teddy bear to her chest as her backpack thumped down the stairs after her. Ryann followed right behind her daughter. She would be strong. Just like always. She was determined to make this fun for Erica.

Glancing over, Ryann saw Stan watching her from his kitchen window two doors down. His glare cut through the space, but she glared right back. She refused to let him see how much he annoyed her, and, frankly, scared her a little. He'd become more persistent in his "requests" lately, which was the biggest factor in Ryann leaving tonight without another place lined up. She had little savings and it would be hard to find an affordable rental in Haven now that the tourist season was fast approaching.

She'd ignored too many red flags about living here for far too long. She was going to have to trust God, something she was trying to do more.

Erica skipped to the car, singing softly under her breath. She climbed into the back seat and settled her things nearby. Erica buckled up Mr. Bear first and then herself.

Ryann tossed her backpack onto the front passenger seat and hurried around to get in. She wanted to be out from under Stan's gaze as quickly as possible.

"Where are we going to go, Mommy?" Erica's little face had such a look of concern on it, that Ryann wanted to turn around and march right back into the trailer and tell Stan to take a flying leap.

Instead, she took a deep breath and said with as much confidence as she could muster, "I don't know, baby, but it will be fun. I promise. God will watch out for us."

Ryann mumbled a prayer, like she always did before she tried starting her fifteen-year-old car. "Lord, please let this old hunk of junk start."

She held her breath as she turned the key. The engine caught and she smiled. She also prayed she wouldn't have to break the promise she had just made to her daughter. No matter what, she would make this fun.

"Let's go on an adventure!" Erica yelled, raising a fist high in the air.

Ryann smiled at her daughter in the rearview mirror, and Erica returned it. "That's the spirit, kiddo! It's going to be fun."

"Bye, house!" Erica waved at the only home she remembered. She didn't remember the house she'd come home to as a baby. Ryann was determined to give her daughter the best life she could as a single mom.

"Let's see where we can find to camp out." Ryann had checked the weather forecast, and the overnight lows were still going to be in the forties. It would be too cold to sleep in the tent. She would need to find a place to park the car that would be out of sight, but safe. She felt anxiety churning in her stomach as she prayed she could keep them both safe.

Pointing the car towards the outskirts of Haven, Ryann drove for about ten minutes before slowing. She was near the old apple orchard outside of town. She could see the rows of trees with their branches curling every which way where they lined the road.

She'd heard Mr. Carruthers, the elderly man who had lived here, had passed away a few weeks ago. She pulled into the driveway and let the car idle as she looked around. The place was dark and had an air of neglect about it. The old barn stood like a sentinel and the house looked like an old soul watching her.

Putting the car in gear, she followed the rutted gravel drive as it circled behind the barn. No one came to confront her for being there.

"Wait here," she told her daughter. Grabbing a flashlight from her backpack, she went to look around. She didn't want to be surprised. Even though it looked like no one was living here, she wanted to be sure.

She could pitch the tent close to the barn, or even in the barn, and convince Erica they were living in the time of Laura Ingalls.

That would excite her daughter. Erica loved the Little House books and had been asking to go out west to see where Laura had lived.

The house proved to be locked up tight. Nothing moved inside, and Ryann felt sure no one was living there. It felt empty.

The barn, however, was not locked. She slid the large barn door open enough to fit her car before driving it right inside. Ryann didn't think anyone would mind her camping on the property. She prayed no one would appear to make her leave.

Deep down, she had the feeling God had led her here. And for now, that was enough. She'd worry about tomorrow when she had to. For now, she would get settled and sell this as the adventure it was to Erica.

"Are we staying here, Mommy?" Erica's eyes shone bright, brighter than they had in a long time.

Ryann often worried on how growing up without a father and then being diagnosed with diabetes would impact her daughter's self-confidence. But so far, her little girl had maintained her cherry outlook on life with barely a missed step. Maybe Ryann needed to follow her daughter's example.

Ryann turned in the seat to answer her daughter. "This is it, sweetie. We're going to pretend we're living in the West with Laura Ingalls as our neighbor. They're just over the ridge. Won't this be fun? No electricity. No water. Just you and me. We'll have to find some of those things tomorrow, but for tonight, we'll sleep here until we can explore a little more. I have tomorrow off from work, so we'll get everything set up. How does that sound?"

The little girl clapped her hands together and squealed, "Yes! I love this adventure, mommy! I can't wait!"

Ryann breathed a sigh of relief. "Let's go explore and see if we can find a place to sleep." She stepped out of the car and opened the back door for Erica. The little girl jumped out and did a little spin.

"This is going to be so much fun!" She took off, skipping down the main aisle of the barn towards a door.

"Hang on, kiddo. Wait for me." Ryann hurried to catch up to where her daughter stood in front of a closed door.

Bouncing on her toes, Erica asked, "What do you think's inside?"

"Let's find out." Ryann grabbed the door handle. The rough door had leather hinges and a piece of curved branch for a handle. Ryann pulled it open and shined her flashlight inside.

Erica wrinkled her nose. "Ewww... something smells!"

Ryann hid the smile that was threatening to bloom on her face. They'd opened the door to a stall that hadn't been cleaned. From the smell of it, something might have even lived there recently. She shut the door.

Ryann smiled down at her daughter. "It's just a stall. An animal lived there, and it needs to be cleaned out. Maybe we can do that tomorrow."

"I bet Laura had to clean stalls."

"I bet she did too, kiddo. Let's keep looking."

The next three doors opened to reveal stalls as well. All needed a good cleaning. Ryann sighed. If they couldn't find a clean space that would work, they might have to sleep in the car tonight. It was at least parked in the barn. Tomorrow would be soon enough to clean out a spot to pitch the tent inside.

"There's one more, Mommy. Do you think it's another stall?"

"Why don't you open the door, and we'll find out."

The little girl heaved on the door with a soft grunt, and it swung open. Ryann shined her flashlight inside and almost dropped it.

Inside the room, a table stood flush against one wall covered in papers as if the person who'd been working there was going to be coming back soon. A set of shelves with miscellaneous jars and cans stood next to it. An oversized twin bed was along the other wall, neatly made with a quilt and pillows. A recliner and a small woodstove rounded out the space.

Aside from the layer of dust, Ryann might have thought Mr. Carruthers was going to show up any minute to kick them out. She couldn't believe her eyes. They wouldn't have to camp in the barn or even sleep in their car. They could stay here.

"Mommy! Are we sleeping here? It doesn't smell as bad as those stalls did."

"We sure are, sweetie. We sure are."

Four

Richard

Richard swallowed a sip of wine, pushing down the nervous feeling that had his belly full of knots. He wanted this night to be perfect, just like the woman sitting across from him. Sloane was a knock-out. She'd caught Richard's eye instantly when they'd first met.

Sloane wasn't the type of woman who would easily accept living in the rural part of the state Richard was now considering. The city was where she thrived. She seemed to gain energy from having lots of people around her. More than once she'd told him how she couldn't wait to move to some place other than Portland. Sloane didn't consider Portland city enough. She had her sights set on New York City, and she wanted to take him with her.

All the same, he was hoping he could convince her to try the plan he'd been working on all afternoon. If he could make the farm viable during the year he was there, he could sell it for a nice profit. With Sloane's connections, he could go back to banking afterwards. He'd be a little behind in his career, but he could catch up easily.

His goal tonight was to convince Sloane to give Haven a year before he gave the rest of his life to making her happy. It would be tricky, but he thought he had a way of presenting it to Sloane that she wouldn't refuse.

Richard knew marriage was the next logical step in their relationship. They'd been dating for over two years. He didn't consider himself a superficial or vain man, but if he were honest with himself, Sloane's looks had been the first thing that had caught his attention.

He loved her wavy blonde hair, stunning blue eyes, and the attention she attracted from other men when they were out together. Even now, Richard's chest swelled with pride at knowing she was his.

Sloane had grand plans for not only her own life, but for his as well. Her level of investment in his career sometimes outmatched his own. And she'd been hinting about marrying him for the last two months. Richard knew she was as ready for this step as he was.

Taking another sip of wine, he slipped his other hand under the table edge to pat his jacket pocket, where Sloane couldn't see. He knew the ring box was there, but he couldn't help checking on it one more time.

They were finishing up the entrée. He knew Sloane would decline dessert. She always did. He planned to suggest they go for a walk along the water. The moon was full tonight. It would be romantic. He would get on one knee and profess his love for her. She would love it. He hoped. It was sometimes hard to tell what Sloane would like.

"Anything exciting happen at work today?" Sloane asked with one perfectly arched eyebrow. "Did you meet with Jacobs over the promotion?"

Surprised, Richard answered without thinking, "I declined it."

The wine glass heading to Sloane's lips stopped midway as her eyes widened briefly before narrowing. She took a deep breath, setting the glass back on the table with a deliberate motion.

"Richard, why did you do something so foolish? The plan was for you to accept the promotion, which would lead to your eventual transfer to New York City. That was the plan. What changed it? I thought we'd agreed." Sloane leaned forward, tapping a long nail twice on the table, one eyebrow raised.

Richard had planned to wait until after the proposal to have this discussion. He'd wanted Sloane in a romantic mood, not an antagonistic one. And he knew the idea of living in Haven would need to be presented with finesse.

Scrambling, he blurted out, "Something happened today. It made me rethink the move to New York right now." He made a fist under the table and tapped his knee. He needed to figure out a way to salvage this situation quickly before the evening ended in a fight.

"What could have happened that was more important than your promotion? Honey, we discussed this. Call Jacobs tomorrow and tell him you changed your mind. I'll talk to Daddy tonight, and he'll make sure it happens. We can fix this."

"There's nothing to fix. I had a complication this afternoon. My great-uncle passed away, and he left me his apple orchard, really his entire estate, in Haven."

"So? What does that have to do with your job? Sell it. We can use the money as a down payment on an apartment in the city." With a sip of her wine, Sloane indicated the discussion was over.

"I can't sell it. Not yet."

"Richard, you're not making any sense."

Richard knew he wasn't. His mind was on how he could save the evening. He took another sip of wine to give himself time to think of how to continue.

"Let me give you the background. I spent most of my summers from the time I was young until I was sixteen working with my great-uncle on his apple farm."

Sloane raised an eyebrow at him. "Manual labor? You? I can't picture it."

"Well, I did. I even wore flannel, jeans, and work boots."

"An outfit I hope to never see on you. Continue."

Richard worked hard to keep the scowl off his face at the interruption before he continued. He picked his words carefully, trying to convey why he was doing all of this. "My great-uncle left me the farm to do with as I wish. The farm has been in my family for generations."

"Sell it," Sloane interrupted again. "Why are we still talking about this?"

"Let me finish, sweetheart." Richard ground out as he tried to keep the irritation out of his voice. He didn't want this conversation to sour his plans, but he felt his irritation continue to rise. "I can't sell it immediately. There was a stipulation in the will."

Richard took a deep breath as he continued. It was now or never. "I need to live there for a year and work the farm. And I need to be there in two weeks. After that, I can sell it if I want to."

"You want to live in Haven and work a farm. You?"

"Yes, me. I know how to run a business. And I know how to run the apple farm." He was losing control of the night, and he wasn't sure how to regain it.

"Richard, be reasonable. You'd make a lousy farmer. You're a brilliant banker. I'll talk to Daddy tonight, and we'll fix this." Sloane sat back in her chair and took another sip from her glass.

"I am being reasonable, Sloane. I want to do this, and I would love for you to come with me."

"Me? There is no way I'm going to live in some little coastal town."

"I made up my mind already this afternoon," Richard said. "That's why I turned down the promotion. I was planning to tell you tonight. In fact," he swallowed hard before continuing, "I gave my notice today. I'm moving to Haven in two weeks, and I want you to come with me. I believe we can make it work."

He knew he was getting ahead of things, but the discussion had pushed his timeline for the night forward. At this point, Richard felt he had nothing left to lose. Maybe a proposal would show her how serious he was about it all–about her, about moving–all of it.

Standing, he reached for the ring box as he slipped to one knee beside her chair. "Sloane, I have..."

Interrupting him again, Sloane hissed, "Get up! Get up right now! Don't you dare do this, Richard Mosely. Not here. Not now. People are looking! Get up!"

She tossed a smile over her shoulder, "It's right there, honey! Just under the table." She laughed, "My earrings are always falling out. Thank you for finding it."

Richard slid back into his chair, surprised at Sloane's reaction. They'd been discussing marriage for months. She'd hinted at the ring she wanted so much he'd had no problem knowing which one she'd wanted. It was the same ring in the box back in his pocket.

Richard was torn between his desires. On the one hand, he knew he loved Sloane. He craved the promotion and big city life. On the other hand, running the apple farm meant dealing with a host of problems, from frost and pests to harvest planning. As he weighed his options, the prospect of sticking to the familiar path crossed his mind, tempting him to abandon the idea of going to Haven.

That was until Sloane rejected him. She hadn't even given it a single thought. While he'd been nervous about asking her to marry him tonight, he hadn't dreamed she'd act that way. Maybe he was wrong about this relationship after all. He was beginning to think maybe his uncle's will had saved him from making a big mistake.

"Richard! Are you listening to me?"

His tone was firm as he spoke. "I'm listening, but I don't think you understand what I'm saying. The truth is, I've already decided to leave Central Bank. I'm going to try making a new life in Haven. And you're welcome to join me."

The minute the words left Richard's mouth, he saw his error. He watched as color flooded Sloane's face. Her eyes narrowed.

"If you've already decided, then why are you here? You must have known I wouldn't go live in some little town in the middle of nowhere. If you leave, we're through, Richard Mosely. Do you hear me?"

"I hear you."

"If you leave, you're going to throw away your career. Daddy won't keep your job for you while you go play at being a farmer. And there's no way I'm going to marry you now, so where will that leave you?"

"I love you, Sloane. But if you can't support me in this so I can support you later, I think it leaves us right here—with you going your way and me heading to Haven alone. I won't beg and I won't change my mind."

Sloane tossed her napkin on the table and stood. "Fine! But mark my words, you'll come crawling back to me sooner rather than later. Richard, farming isn't in your blood. You're a professional, a banker. Too bad you aren't acting like one." She tossed her hair over her shoulder and walked away without a backwards glance.

Richard worked to control his temper as the waiter hurried over to him.

"Are you ready to leave, sir? Was everything to your liking?"

"Yes, and everything was fine. My girlfriend," he tried not to grimace at the word, "just needed some air."

"Very good. I'll be right back with your check."

Richard watched the man hurry away. He knew he could have been happy working his way up the corporate ladder, living in the city, and marrying Sloane, but now he had another option. He wanted to see where it would take him. The decision just felt right.

His mind drifted to all the things he needed to do before heading to Haven. He didn't know what he'd find when he got to the farm, but he hoped his Uncle Art had left the house in a livable condition. He was feeling eager at the opportunity ahead of him.

Some might say he was having an early mid-life crisis, but Richard was looking forward to seeing where his new life would lead. An apple orchard. In Haven. The possibilities were endless.

Five

N o...no...no." Ryann muttered under her breath as her car made horrible gasping and rattling noises just as she pulled into the barn that night. She knew little about cars, but she knew enough to realize it was making sounds that weren't normal.

Two weeks ago, she'd moved out to the farm. The room they'd found that first night was a perfect little hideaway. It hadn't taken long to clean out the dust and old things. The bed was just big enough for them. The room was far cozier than staying in the car.

Even though Erica was still excited about the adventure of living on the farm, Ryann wasn't as enthusiastic about it. Still, she kept up appearances for her daughter. The extra work of staying hidden was taking a toll on her. She was sure the bags under her eyes had grown since they'd moved in.

There was an outhouse in the back corner of the barn that was still usable. Although Ryann shuddered at remembering the spider which had greeted her one morning. She'd been half asleep when she'd pushed the door open. The arachnid had been hanging at face height. She'd almost swallowed the thing after gasping in shock. She'd ducked with flailing arms to make sure it hadn't landed on her. Since that day, she kept a broom nearby and opened the door carefully, weapon ready to sweep away anything dark and fuzzy.

Erica had jumped with joy when they'd found the old hand pump tucked behind the barn. Her daughter had volunteered to pump the water to see if it still worked. The water had flowed after only a few hard pumps, which surprised Ryann.

They could stay clean with sponge baths. They used the stove at night to heat the water as well as to take the chill out of the air. The darkness hid any smoke rising above the tree line. Erica loved how they heated the water on the stove and used a basin of warm water to wipe down. Washing their hair was harder, but doable. Ryann longed for an actual shower.

Her stubborn streak was the one thing holding Ryann back from asking for help. She'd been contemplating asking the ladies she worked for if they knew of anywhere she could rent. Brenda, Colleen, and Abigail probably knew at least three or four options just off the top of their heads, but she couldn't bring herself to ask. She should be able to provide for her daughter on her own.

Ryann hated they were staying somewhere they didn't have permission to be. Homeless. Squatting. She knew she was letting her pride get in the way, yet here she was anyway. She prayed God, and whoever owned the land now, would forgive her.

She hadn't been to church since she'd left the trailer and arrived at the farm. She couldn't face Pastor Peter and the others at church, knowing she was doing something wrong. Sighing, she laid her head against the steering wheel and once more prayed, even though it seemed God was so far away lately.

"God, I can't do this anymore. I just can't." Her voice trailed off as silent tears ran down her cheeks. She quickly wiped them away, hoping Erica wouldn't notice. She needed to be strong for her little girl.

With the car giving her problems, they would now have to walk wherever they needed to go. It wasn't like she could ask for a ride, considering she didn't want anyone to know where she was staying. And walking would take up valuable time and energy she needed to care for herself and, more importantly, her daughter.

Maybe the Lord was listening. After all, she'd limped her vehicle into the barn before it had given a loud backfire and shuddered to a stop.

Ryann let her head fall back against the headrest as she whispered, "Lord, why? What are you trying to teach me here?"

"What's wrong, Mommy?" Erica's innocent voice floated forward from the back seat.

Ryann worked to hold back the tears she felt rising once more. She didn't have time to cry. At least she had tomorrow off. She'd have time to figure out what to do.

The sisters were being so great about letting Erica come to the restaurant since Ryann had found no one willing to babysit. Her daughter wasn't pleased with the arrangement, but Brenda had changed her mind when she offered to teach Erica how to bake.

On top of living on a farm like Laura Ingalls, Erica was now learning how to bake bread, cookies, scones, and hand pies. She thought life couldn't get much better. While Ryann wasn't thriving, it was clear her daughter was. Maybe even more than she ever had before.

"Mommy?" She felt her little girl climb over the seat and curl up beside her, snuggling into her side. Given that Ryann's little Honda Civic was nearly twenty years old and had almost three hundred thousand miles on it, it wasn't surprising that it was giving her troubles. Although, it had been reliable up until this point. She wasn't sure what to do now.

"I'm okay, pretty girl. It's just been a long day."

"Mommy, I'm feeling a little dizzy."

Pushing down the quick rise of panic, Ryann looked at her daughter. She didn't want to jump to the worse case scenario, but it was hard not to. She couldn't help but ask, "When did you check your sugar last?"

"I don't remember."

"Give me your backpack, sweetie."

"I don't wanna climb in the back."

Ryann watched as her daughter curled up on the seat. Erica closed her eyes and her breathing increased. Ryann opened her door, jumped out, and ripped opened the back door. Grabbing her daughter's backpack from where it lay on the floor, she hurried around to the passenger side. "Hang on, kiddo."

Opening her daughter's door, Ryann squatted down in front of her and placed a hand on her forehead. Erica felt a little clammy. Unzipping the backpack, Ryann pulled out the testing kit. She popped a test strip into the meter. "Give me your hand, Erica."

Lazily, her daughter rolled her head to look at her and floated a hand towards her mother. Grabbing it, Ryann pulled it closer. "Just a little pinch..." Using the lancet, Ryann squeezed out a drop of blood and loaded the test strip. The five seconds it took to get a reading seemed to take forever.

"Hurry! Hurry!" she whispered. She worked to control her anxiety as she felt her heart racing. Her mind was whirling with all the things she should do.

The number popped up-55. Ryann bit back the curse on the tip of her lips at the number. She rooted through her daughter's bag, praying there was a juice box handy. She felt the cardboard and pulled it out, giving it a shake. It was full. "Thank God! Erica, drink this. Come on, baby."

"What? I don't wanna." Erica looked at her with unfocused eyes.

Ryann didn't bother to argue with her daughter. Quickly popping the straw into the container, she placed the straw between the little girl's lips, holding it there. "Drink."

Without arguing, Erica sucked down the sweet juice. With her other hand, Ryann rummaged around in the bag for another juice box. She came up empty.

Slurping noises came as Erica reached the bottom of the drink. Ryann knew she should give the juice time to work, but she hated how long it could take.

She rummaged again in the bag, looking to see what she could find. Whoever had come up with the 15/15 rule of eat 15 carbs and wait 15 minutes had clearly never had a child with a rapidly decreasing blood sugar.

Her hand wrapped around a squished granola bar in the bottom of the bag. "Eat this, too, baby." She unwrapped the bar and handed it over.

Erica reached out a clumsy hand and grabbed the bar, munching slowly on it.

Ryann glanced at her watch to see how much time had passed–only five minutes. It seemed like forever.

"Mommy, what's that noise?"

Ryann had been so focused on her daughter that she'd missed the sound of tires on gravel. Someone was pulling into the driveway.

Six

Richard sighed with relief as he pulled into the dooryard at his uncle's farm. Putting the car in park, he sat as he took in the inheritance sitting in front of him. He was now the proud owner of an apple farm, complete with a house, a barn, and multiple outbuildings. The last two weeks had been a whirlwind of activity.

While he was eager to start his new adventure, he wasn't ready to do it without a backup plan. It had taken time to find someone to sublet his apartment for the next year. He wanted the option to return to Portland if things didn't work out in Haven.

His only regret was how he'd ended it with Sloane. He'd thought proposing might help move their relationship forward. At least, that had been the impression she'd given him. But that had all been a colossal failure.

Sighing, he closed his eyes as he remembered her visit last night. She'd shown up as he finished packing. The conversation hadn't gone well.

"I see you're still planning to go." Sloane stood with arms crossed, tapping her foot as disapproval radiated from her.

"I am." Richard kept packing. He knew he needed to tell her things were over. Before he could start, she came to stand in front of him.

"And I can't talk you out of it?" She reached out a finger, drawing it down the front of his shirt, smiling up at him.

Normally that would be enough to get his heart racing, and he would do anything she asked. But now he took her hand, removing it. She'd hurt him more than he'd realized when she'd rejected his proposal.

While he still found her attractive, he'd realized he didn't really love Sloane. Not like he should if he was going to commit his life to her. He'd recognized he was only with her for the boost she could give to his career. And, he hated to admit it, some fear at what she could also do to his career if they broke up.

Leaving for Haven was giving him the perfect excuse to break things off. If he ended up back in banking at the end of the year, he could restart his career on his terms rather than on how Sloane wanted him to act.

"Sloane, I'm going to Haven tomorrow. And I'm excited about this new adventure."

She pouted at his words. Another method that had worked in the past to get him to change his mind. She opened her mouth to speak.

Richard held up a hand. "Maybe it's better if we just ended this. We don't want the same things right now. I think you'd be happier if you moved on and found someone more compatible."

Sloane's brows narrowed in anger. Her voice was tight as she responded, "Richard, you're going to regret doing this. No one leaves me. No one."

Spinning on her heel, she walked out the door, slamming it behind her. Richard winced even now at the memory of it. Although, there was also a feeling of relief. For the first time in a long time, he felt like he could make his own decisions without worrying about how Sloane would react to it.

Getting out of his truck, Richard stood and stretched. Despite the fading light, he thought there was time to take a quick look around the farm before it was too dark. He would have been here sooner, but he'd forgotten what the roads were like. Google had said it would take an hour and a half, but it had taken an extra thirty minutes due to slow drivers and potholes.

Stepping around the holes in the steps, he cautiously put his weight on the front porch. It seemed firm. Striding to the front door, he gave the doorknob a twist. Locked. Huh. The lawyer handling his grandfather's estate had said nothing about needing a key and hadn't included one with the final paperwork, either. Richard had just assumed the building would be open. During all his visits, Richard had never seen his uncle lock the house.

Standing with his hands on his hips, Richard turned to survey his surroundings. The barn was to the left. A storage shed nearby caught his attention. His uncle used to store his lawn tools there, and he wondered if there might be something inside that would help open the door. He hurried towards the shed.

He hit the metal tab to open the door latch and pulled. The squeak of hinges sounded loud in his ears with all the quiet surrounding him. Uncle Art lived a couple miles outside Haven. His acreage ensured he had no neighbors. Richard heard only the gurgling of a stream running nearby and a few insects serenading the end of the day as the sun continued to dip towards the horizon.

Pulling out his cell phone, he tapped open the flashlight. He held it high and looked inside the dark shed. Uncle Art had all his tools hanging neatly on the walls or tucked under the workbench nearby. Orderly, as always. He stepped inside. Turning, he noticed a key hanging on a hook near the door.

On a hunch, Richard took the key and hurried back across the overgrown lawn to the front door. He slipped the key in the lock. It turned smoothly. Go figure. Even though the house was locked, the key to open it was in an unlocked shed.

Pushing the door open, he coughed as a slight breeze caused dust to swirl up. He reached for the light switch he knew was inside the door, flipping it on. Nothing.

Just as he'd remembered, the front door opened into the living room. Uncle Art's old recliner still sat there. Beside it was a table piled high with seed catalogs, farming magazines, and novels. Uncle Art had been an avid reader. Richard knew the next room used to be full of shelves loaded with books.

Sure enough, inside the den, bookshelves covered the walls. His uncle had books shoved in everywhere on the shelves and piled on the floor. Uncle Art never got rid of a book once it crossed the threshold of his house. "They're like old friends. How could I get rid of any?"

Richard chuckled to himself. Now he'd be stuck going through them all. He doubted he would save many. He didn't feel the same way about books as his uncle had. Besides, he wouldn't have much time to read this year. Not if he wanted to make sure the farm turned a profit.

Walking along one shelf, Richard ran his fingers along the titles. His uncle had liked a variety of genres and the titles reflected that. There were a few Louis L'Amour, some Clive Cussler, and lots of Tom Clancy. He even had Diana Gabaldon, Lee Childs, and James Patterson. He noticed a few Francine Rivers and Terri Blackstock as well.

He headed towards the first-floor bedroom. There was a queen-sized bed between two windows. A quilt, all browns and whites with some red, still covered it. He recalled his uncle telling him how his great-great grandmother had made it. It was one of the items she'd brought with her when she immigrated from England in the late-1800s.

He crossed the room and opened the door to the small half-bath he'd helped his uncle add one summer. "I'm tired of walking clear across the house to use the head. Seems like we don't need all this closet space. Let's see what we can do." It looked the same, just more tired and dirty. Like the rest of the house.

Going back into the bedroom, he crossed the room and went out a different door. He was now in the kitchen. He could walk from one room to the other on the first floor without ever going into a hallway.

In the kitchen, he ran his hand over the big, black, old-fashioned cookstove still taking up half of one wall. The slate sink took up most of another. While his uncle had running water, whoever had added plumbing to the house had kept the hand pump at one end of the sink. They'd simply retrofitted it to act as the faucet. Richard remembered being completely fascinated by it when he visited.

The door to the backyard was off to the left side of the stove. He walked over to check it. Sure enough, the deadbolt was closed. He stood in the kitchen, hands on his hips as he looked around.

Everything seemed as if his uncle had simply gone to town and would be back at any moment. It was all neat and put away. Other than a layer of dust, the house looked capable of housing Richard.

He nodded. He could camp out inside tonight. Calling the electric company to get the electricity back on would be his priority tomorrow morning. Then he could tackle cleaning the place out. The size of that job was overwhelming.

He rubbed a hand through his hair. Unless he found some help, there was no way he'd ever succeed. His uncle had lived here for over fifty years. No wonder Uncle Art had given him a year to work the farm. Just going through the house contents would take that much time, let alone getting the orchard up and running as well.

"You never did things the easy way, Uncle Art," he mumbled to himself while heading out to fetch his bag.

Excitement filled him at the thought of bringing the farm back to working order. He planned out what he'd need to tackle tomorrow once he took care of the essentials—like electricity. He would need to assess inventory, formulate a business plan, and write up a budget. One step at a time. He could do this.

He grabbed his duffel bag off the back seat of his car. Then snagged his computer bag out of the front, slinging the strap over his shoulder. He snatched the bag of food he'd picked up in town and went back into the house. Mentally, he began running through what he'd need to take care of first thing in the morning to make the house livable.

Until then, he remembered there was an outhouse in the barn. Well, if he was going to embrace the rustic life until he had electricity, maybe he should go all in. He smiled.

Dropping his duffle bag on the couch, he went into the kitchen. He deposited his laptop bag on the table along with the food. Making sure he had his phone, he headed out to the barn to see if the outhouse was still usable.

Despite the house being locked, the barn was not. He yanked open the side door and stopped short. There was a car in his barn. A car with no dust on it. A car that looked like it didn't quite belong.

Cautiously, he started inside. The tall windows let in a little light, but dusk was falling. While it was dim in the barn, he could see where he was going without the need of his flashlight. Although the corners stayed darker than he would like.

Stepping quietly, Richard walked around the vehicle. He put his hand on the hood. It was warm to the touch. Who was on his property?

"Hello?" he called. "Anyone here?"

He peeked in the car windows as he walked around it, keeping an eye out for any movement. There was a backpack on the back seat. He tried opening a door. Locked.

"I won't hurt you. Show yourself!"

He turned toward the back of the barn where his uncle used to have a room. He would hang out there, relaxing between chores, or hiding from his wife. Aunt Carol didn't take any guff from anyone, especially her husband. She had strong opinions and wasn't shy about sharing them. "I just need a little alone time," Uncle Art had told Richard one day when he'd found him reading in front of the woodstove in his hideaway room.

Starting towards the back room to investigate, Richard caught a flash of light from under the door. There was a furious whispering of words, but they were too low for him to make out what was being said or how many people were in there. It was likely teenagers thinking they had found a make out spot.

Richard stomped a foot twice and yelled, "I can hear you!"

The words cut off.

"I'm coming in. I won't hurt you," he called again. Taking a deep breath, he put his hand on the latch, easing the door open.

Huddled on the bed was a woman who looked like she was in her late twenties or early thirties. He was never good at pinpointing a woman's age. The woman had her arms wrapped around a young girl, who stared at him with bleary eyes.

"Who are you?" Richard demanded.

Seven

R yann gasped as the door swung open. She'd wanted to run as soon as she'd heard the tires on the gravel, but Erica was still woozy from the low blood sugar. The food she'd eaten hadn't kicked in fast enough for her to have the strength to escape with Ryann through the woods. And really, where else could she go?

"Just let us leave. We don't want any trouble." Ryann tightened her arms around her daughter. "She doesn't feel good. Just give us another ten minutes, and we'll be out of your way."

"Who are you? What are you doing here? What's wrong with her?"

The questions flew at Ryann so fast she didn't know where to start. A man stood framed in the doorway. He was wearing a pair of dark jeans and work boots. He had on a black t-shirt with an untucked red and black flannel over the top of it. Somehow, the clothing didn't quite fit with the rest of his manicured looks. It was almost as if he was trying out a role.

Tackling the last question first, she stated, "Nothing. She has diabetes. She's recovering from a low sugar. We just need a few more minutes for the sugar she ate to hit her bloodstream. Then we'll be out of your hair."

At the words, Ryann glanced at the man's head. That was it. His hair was too perfect. Men who wore work boots and flannel didn't wear their hair slicked back with whatever he was using. The polished look screamed city-boy while the clothing said country-boy.

Ryann went on the offense. "And who are you, and what are you doing here?" She didn't know who this man was, but what if he had no more right to be here than she did? She raised an eyebrow at him as she waited for his answer.

"I own the place. I'm Richard, Richard Mosely. This was my uncle's farm. Your turn. You didn't tell me who you are or why you're here."

Richard? This man couldn't be Ricky. Ryann held her breath. She used to hang out with him when he came to visit his uncle on the farm. She hadn't seen him since they were sixteen. Would he remember her? Maybe. She didn't think she'd changed all that much over the last fourteen years, but then again, she hadn't recognized him at first glance either.

"It's a long story. The short version is my landlord kicked me out over a bogus issue. I didn't have any place to go. I was driving by looking for a place to camp. The farm looked abandoned, so I thought we could stay here until I could figure out a better option. Like I said, we'll get out of here as soon as my daughter is okay to walk." Ryann let her words slow. She was giving too much away.

Her stomach dropped at the thought of having to walk any-where with Erica tonight. Thankfully, they had accumulated little beyond what they'd brought with them over the last two weeks of staying here. Once again, they would leave with their backpacks only.

But where would they go? Maybe it was time to swallow her pride and ask for help at work. She knew Abigail and the rest would help her if they knew. Ryann felt tears slipping down her cheeks.

"Hey," Richard stepped further into the room, "we'll figure out something."

Ryann tensed for a moment as he filled the already small room. She wasn't used to having a man around. Richard seemed to loom over where Ryann and Erica sat on the bed. And yet, she didn't feel intimidated by him.

Erica wiggled in Ryann's arms. "Mommy, you're squashing me."

"Oh, sorry, sweetheart." Ryann loosened the tight hold she had on Erica. "Are you feeling better?"

The little girl nodded her head.

"Let me check your sugar." Ryann stood, forcing Richard to take a step back towards the door. She scooped the testing kit off the table and hurried back to Erica.

Quickly placing a test strip in the monitor, Ryann clicked the lancet against Erica's finger. She scooped up the bead of blood needed, and the two heads bent over the monitor, waiting. The number popped up. 110.

"It looks like you're doing better." Ryann kissed her daughter on the top of the head. "Why don't you go grab a package of peanut butter crackers? I'll give you a shot for them in a second. And there should be a bottle of water over there, too. Drink that."

"Okay, Mommy." Erica hopped off the bed and scurried over to grab the snack and drink.

She waved a small hand at Richard, "Hi!" completely unconcerned with the large man standing just inside the door.

Ryann closed her eyes for a moment before standing to face Richard. She'd grown tired of feeling like he was looming over her. It didn't help that he'd filled out considerably since she'd last seen him. He was no longer a lanky teenager.

There was a scruff of beard on his cheeks. She liked it. She'd always liked a man with facial hair. It made them appear, well, more manly. She rolled her eyes at herself before turning to face him.

"We'll be out of here as soon as we can. Sorry, we moved in without permission. I heard Art had passed away, so I thought it would be okay. We've only been out in the barn and..." She let her words die before she rambled further.

Rubbing a hand over her face, she gave him an apologetic smile before continuing. "My car died when I got here tonight. We'll walk into town tomorrow and I'll get someone to come get it." It seemed like it was finally time to ask Brenda and the rest for help.

Ryann flushed slightly under Richard's gaze. She hadn't meant to stay so long, but the barn had felt like home–oddly enough. She knew it had been too good to last.

"Is it okay if we stay the night? I don't want my daughter having to walk so far right now."

Town was about two miles away. Walking after having a low blood sugar might cause Erica to go low again. Ryann didn't want to be caught on the road after dark with her daughter having another low blood sugar.

"Otherwise, just give us time for her to eat her snack." Ryann knew she was babbling and snapped her mouth shut.

If they left now, she'd just skip the shot, which should keep her daughter's blood sugar stable. Erica would love the adventure of walking in the dark. Ryann thought Brenda would let them stay at her place until they could find somewhere else to go.

Richard cleared his throat. "Would you let me put you up in a hotel tonight? I can get your car towed and looked at as well."

Ryann's eyes widened at Richard's offer. It took her a minute to gather her thoughts. "I couldn't let you go to all that trouble. I'm the one here where I shouldn't be. We'll be gone as soon as possible."

She walked over to where Erica was sitting, her mind racing. She prayed silently. *Lord, help make it clear what we should do. Keep us safe.*

"I have another idea," Richard said.

Ryann turned back, willing herself to wait for him to speak. She placed a hand on Erica's shoulder. Her daughter, oblivious to everything around her, was eating her snack while reading one of her Laura books.

"My uncle lived here for fifty plus years. He's collected a lot of things. The house appears to have gone with no updates for years. I'm planning to stay for a while to get things ready to sell. I'll let you stay on the farm if you'll help me do all that."

Ryann narrowed her eyes at him as she considered his words. She wouldn't consider Richard a stranger, but she didn't know what type of man the boy she'd once been friends with had grown up to be. Did he have integrity? What would he want in exchange for her help?

She raised an eyebrow at him. "How much?"

Richard looked at her with confusion. "How much what?"

"How much to do that? What do you want from me?"

He took a step closer, a smile on his face. "I wasn't clear, was I. In exchange for your help, you can stay here rent free. It will only cost you labor. It's a win-win. You get a place to stay with your daughter, and I get help cleaning out my uncle's house."

"That seems a little too good to be true."

"You haven't seen inside the house yet. It's going to take a lot of work. I also need to get the orchard up and going again. I'm going to need all the help I can get."

"What else might you want from me?" She raised an eyebrow at him. "Because the answer is no."

Holding up his hands, Richard said, "I'm not that kind of guy. Strictly business. You help me sort, haul, and clean the house for starters. In exchange, you and your daughter can have the second floor of the house. If I remember right, there are three bedrooms up there, as well as a full bathroom. We can share the kitchen."

Ryann looked at him in confusion. "Why don't you just hire someone to clean the place out and move on? There are companies you could hire that would do it faster." She looked at his hair, at his boots, and back at his eyes. "You don't strike me as someone used to manual labor."

Richard's cheeks flushed as he looked at Ryann, clearly taken aback by her words. Ryann couldn't tell if he was angry or embarrassed, but either way, she found the expression made him more approachable. She made a mental note to be careful around him, as she couldn't deny she found the grown-up Richard far too attractive for her own good.

"Look, I used to come spend summers with my uncle. I know how to work even if it doesn't look like it. But my uncle had a sense of humor." Richard gave a dry chuckle before continuing. "If I want to sell the place, I need to live here for a year and bring the orchard back up to speed. Otherwise, I'll forfeit it all to the fire department for training. I'd hate to see all of this burned down."

Ryann nodded her head in agreement. During her two-week stay in the barn, she'd grown to appreciate its history. Although she'd be happy to move out of their rustic quarters and back into a place with a flush toilet and a bed she didn't have to share with her daughter. Her daughter who kicked in her sleep more than Ryann realized.

She glanced over at where Erica was sitting and eating at the small table while she read. Her daughter would love living in the farmhouse. Just like Laura.

"Okay, you've got a deal." Ryann glanced again at her daughter and then raised an eyebrow at Richard. "Strictly business. Nothing else"

Ryann held out her hand to shake Richard's. He grasped hers, and Ryann felt a jolt of pleasure shoot up her arm. Maybe this wasn't a good idea after all.

"Now that we have a deal, how about you tell me your name?" Richard raised his perfectly groomed eyebrows at her as he let go of her hand.

Ryann took a breath. Time to find out if he would remember her from all those summers ago.

"Ricky, it's me, Ryann."

Eight

S tunned, Richard stared at the woman in front of him. This couldn't be the same Ryann he used to tear around the orchard with, could it? He'd met her the first summer he'd arrived on his uncle's farm. He was eight years old, painfully shy, and so homesick all he could do was sit on the porch, watching for his parents to return.

One afternoon he'd seen a girl about his age walking up the road, kicking a rock and whistling. Ryann had worn her hair in two braided pigtails that hung almost to her waist. She'd spotted him, bolting towards the porch before skidding to a stop in front of him.

Richard still remembered that first conversation.

Panting slightly, Ryann had asked, "Wanna go play in the field?"

"No."

"Why not?"

"Cause."

"Cause why?" She'd scratched her nose and left a streak of dirt behind.

Richard had squinted at her. "Cause I don't. I'm waiting for my parents. I don't want to miss them."

His aunt had pushed the screen door open at that point and shooed him off. That was the day he'd learned how much fun there was to run in the fields, get dirty, and, most importantly, have a friend.

Every summer after that, he'd sought Ryann out as soon as he'd arrived. He had so many memories of working in the orchard with her nearby. His favorites were when they'd been older and could finally go to the creek without an adult. They'd spent hours down there building dams, having splash fights, hunting frogs, and fishing.

The last time he'd seen Ryann, it was the summer they'd turned sixteen. It was the summer he realized she was no longer a tomboy. It was the summer he realized he liked her as more than just a friend. He'd tried to get up the courage to kiss her before she'd left. He always regretted the fact he'd never managed it.

Shaking off the memories, he glanced at the little girl sitting at the table, eating and reading her book. There was a little resemblance to Ryann. Enough that he would consider them related. He couldn't help but glance at Ryann's ring finger. No ring. Was she married? Divorced? He had so many questions.

When his parents moved the year he turned 17, he'd lost touch with Ryann. He'd always wished he'd had the courage to ask his uncle about her, but he never had.

Richard couldn't see the freckles he remembered on Ryann's face, and her long brown hair was now tied up in a high ponytail.

"So, how have you been?" Richard kicked himself mentally. What kind of question was that? He hadn't seen her in over a decade and, after finding her squatting in his uncle's barn, that's the first thing he asked her? He was an idiot.

"I've been better." Ryann stood to her fullest height, which he realized brought her just level with his chin.

"Again, I'm sorry we ended up here. Trust me, this wasn't my first choice of places to live with my daughter. My only other choice was my car." She gave a rueful glance towards the open doorway behind him. "But that just died on me as I pulled into the barn tonight." She waved a hand as if to bat away the words. "I'm sorry. I'll get us out of here as soon as I can."

"It's okay. You only startled me. I wasn't expecting to find anyone here."

"Thanks. Like I said earlier, I'll talk to someone tomorrow about it."

"Sure. Why don't you and Erica, was it? Why don't you grab what you need for the night and come on inside? We'll see what the upstairs bedrooms look like and get you settled in the house."

As Richard watched Ryann mull over his proposal, he couldn't help but feel a twinge of anxiety. He hoped she would say yes. Reconnecting would help take his mind off all he'd left behind to follow this career change. And if she was still as carefree as she had been during those summers, well, then he could use a little more carefree spirit in his life.

"If you don't mind, I think we'll spend tonight here. It's important for things to be..." she glanced at where Erica had finished her snack and was now engrossed in her book. "Well, to be normal. We're used to this room, so we'll stay here tonight. I don't want to move her right before bedtime."

Richard nodded. "I understand. How long has she been sick?"

Ryann shot him a glare.

"Did I say something wrong? She is sick, right?"

"No, she isn't sick. Not like you mean. She has diabetes. She was diagnosed a few months ago and we're still working out some things."

"I didn't mean to upset you. I'm sorry," Richard said as he shoved his hands in his pockets. He wasn't an awkward teenager anymore. He needed to remember that.

Ryann sighed. "You didn't. I'm the one who's sorry. It's been a rollercoaster of a long day. I didn't mean to take it out on you."

"Have you had dinner yet?"

Ryann shook her head and glanced at her daughter. "I was planning to warm some soup on the camp stove."

Richard glanced to the corner where Ryann pointed. He saw a neat area of groceries stacked on the clean workbench. The meals were uncomplicated, able to be eaten either chilled or heated over the camp stove, which was placed on a few bricks close to the window.

Hoping Ryann would agree, Richard said, "Come join me in the house. I picked up some things in town. Nothing fancy, but I think I can manage sandwiches." He made himself stop talking. He didn't want to frighten Ryann away, and he didn't want to appear like a stalker. They'd been friends once. He hoped they could reconnect, share some memories.

"We're good with the soup. Thanks anyway."

"Soup *and* sandwiches. Sounds like a perfect meal. C'mon." Richard held out a hand to her. "Join me. We can make a game plan on how to tackle the work to get this place livable. It will be a working supper."

Richard waited while Ryann considered the offer. She glanced at his outstretched hand. He continued to hold it out, waiting to see if she would take it. It had been impulsive, but he didn't want to take it back now.

He wasn't sure what was wrong with him. He never used to be so impulsive in anything. Ever since he'd inherited Saltwater Orchard from his uncle, he had been deciding faster than he'd ever had in his life.

He normally thought everything through. There was something about this woman in front of him that made him want to help her. Maybe it was all the memories that had flooded in when he'd realized who she was. She'd helped him once when he was feeling lonely. Something in her eyes said she might feel the same way. If he could make that better for her like she had for him, he wanted to do that.

"Okay," Ryann said as she took his hand.

Richard felt something warm fill his stomach at her touch. He held her hand a moment longer than he needed to, but he couldn't seem to let go. Giving it a squeeze, he forced himself to release it. He took a step back as he said, "Good. Can I carry anything?"

"It's just a can of soup. I can manage."

Richard heard the humor in Ryann's voice, and he was sure she was trying to hide a smile.

"Erica," Ryann called to her daughter, "grab your book. We're going to the farmhouse for dinner."

Her little girl kept her head bent, engrossed in her reading. Richard smiled as he saw the exasperation on Ryann's face.

"Erica!" Ryann snapped her fingers to get her daughter's attention.

Erica's head popped up at the noise. "Sorry, Mommy. Laura just lost her dog. It's so sad. Can I have a puppy?"

Richard looked from Erica to Ryann, eyes wide. That was a quick topic change. He heard a giggle, and he glanced at Ryann. Sure enough, she had her hand over her mouth, hiding a smile.

"Are all kids like that?"

"You get used to it," Ryann said as she gave him a smile. His breath caught. She was far more beautiful than he remembered.

Ryann walked over to the shelf to grab the soup. "C'mon, kiddo. We're going to go have supper with Mr. Richard. He has sandwiches and we'll have some soup, too. And no, you can't have a dog. Now grab your book and your insulin kit and let's go."

"We get to go in the house?" Erica's eyes went wide at the thought. "No way!" She clapped her hands together before doing as Ryann had instructed.

Richard headed out the door to wait for them. It seemed too intimate to stand in the room as they gathered their things. He waited next to the car and smiled at the two of them as they soon joined him.

Turning, he led the way to the house. He slowed his steps so Erica wouldn't have to run to keep pace. Richard kept glancing at Ryann as they crossed the yard. He was curious to know what had caused her to end up a single mom living in his barn with her young daughter.

And he wanted to know who Erica's father was. And, more importantly, where he was. He felt anger ripple through him at the thought of the man abandoning his family. He should be here providing for Ryann and Erica, so they weren't living in a car or a barn or anywhere but a warm, safe house.

Glancing at Ryann again, Richard realized he wanted to get to know this older version of Ryann. He wanted to know if there was a place in her life for him, like there had been once. As a friend. She looked like she could use one and so could he.

Nine

Ryann

Ryann wasn't sure what she'd been thinking. Well, she knew what she'd been thinking. She was thinking she was desperate and homeless and living in a barn with no electricity.

Ryann glanced at Richard, walking confidently beside her toward the farmhouse. She was having a hard time making the memory she had of the little boy, who had once dared her to climb to the top of the big pine tree behind the barn, to this man. Richard seemed too sophisticated. How was he going to manage running an apple farm?

When she'd first met Ricky, he was a shy little boy. Ryann had been full of life and loved getting dirty. She'd practically dragged him along with her. He'd soon learned to love the outdoors as much as she did.

The older version of Ricky, the one she remembered from the last summer she'd seen him, had been adorable with his tousled hair and still shy grin. But this adult version, she couldn't get it to mesh. This Richard seemed too buttoned-up, too professional, too... well, too citified.

Ryan had to say something. The silence was feeling awkward. She needed to shake off the old memories and get to know this man, especially if she was going to work for him. "I'm sorry to hear about your uncle. I have some wonderful memories of Mr. Carruthers."

"Thanks. Me too. I used to love spending summers here with him and Aunt Carol." He stopped walking and pivoted to face her. "And you. I liked my summers with you, too."

He turned back and pulled the door open before Ryann could react. She'd liked the summers she'd spent with him as well. But that had been a long time ago, and a lot had changed since then.

She grabbed her daughter's hand as they followed Richard into the house. The fading light of the evening made it hard to see. She stayed close behind as Richard wove his way through the front room towards the kitchen at the back of the house. Her memories of running in and out of the kitchen to snag chocolate chip cookies hot out of the oven overwhelmed her. Those had been good times, now long gone.

"Hang on and I'll get some light."

"Mommy! It's just like when Laura was alive!"

Ryann felt her daughter bouncing on her toes in excitement beside her. She wasn't sure how she'd ever convince Erica to go back to the barn tonight to sleep. Especially if the little girl found out they would move into the house.

Richard turned on two electric lanterns. Placing one in the center of the table, he hung the other one off a cabinet near a wood cookstove.

"It shouldn't take me long to get this started. We can heat the soup on here and take the chill off. Give me a second." Richard rummaged in a cabinet, muttering to himself.

"Aha!" He held up a long lighter as he turned around. "Now let's see what we have for fuel."

Fumbling in the wood box nearby, he pulled out a handful of kindling and began laying the wood in the stove. Richard clicked the lighter once, twice, and on the third time, he exclaimed, "There!"

He fanned the flame carefully with his hand until Ryann could see it growing from where she was standing across the room.

"I have made fire!" Richard called out as he turned with a flourish, bowing as Erica began to laugh and clap.

Ryann couldn't help but laugh along with her daughter. "Well, done, Robinson Caruso."

Richard chuckled as he replaced the cover on the opening in the stove. "There are some pots and pans around here somewhere. I'm planning to make a run to town tomorrow to get cleaning supplies and whatever else we might need. Maybe we can make a list over supper."

Ryann's stomach clenched with emotion as Richard spoke. The low lighting added to the intimacy of the moment, making her feel like they were on a date. But she knew better. She was just being fanciful. She hadn't seen Richard in fourteen years. This wasn't a date or anything even resembling one. She needed to be practical and keep her emotions in check.

"You *are* going to get the electricity turned on, right? I mean, this is fun and all, but I don't think we'll be able to make much progress without it. Water would be good, too." Ryann began opening the cupboards, looking for a pan to put the soup in.

"Top of my list for tomorrow. I'm just not sure how long it will take."

Richard moved to the counter beside Ryann and began unpacking the groceries he'd brought. He laid out bread, lunchmeat, cheese, mayonnaise, and mustard. "I have fixings for ham and cheese sandwiches. What kind of soup do you have?"

"I don't know. I just grabbed the first can I saw." Ryann picked up the can and held it closer to the light to read the label. "Looks like I grabbed tomato. Do you have any butter? I can make some grilled cheese to go with them instead of ham sandwiches."

"Indeed, I do. And I love grilled cheese sandwiches and tomato soup. Especially when I get to eat it with two pretty ladies." He winked at Ryann.

Ryann flushed, hoping the low lighting would hide it. It seemed she needed to make some more ground rules. She needed to make sure Richard understood exactly what it was she was offering.

Turning and placing her hands on her hips, she began, "Look, let's make one thing clear."

"Do you live here?" Erica interrupted as she wandered over to the large iron cookstove. The fire inside already had the place cozy.

Two doors flanked the stove, one leading to the attached shed and the other to the backyard. Ryann wondered if the screen door was still there to give a satisfying slap. It had done just that when she and Ricky had darted in for a quick snack or drink when they were younger.

Richard didn't even glance at Ryann before walking over to Erica. "I do. My uncle used to live here, but he passed away. He left his house and farm to me."

"I'm sorry your uncle died. My daddy died, too."

Ryann felt her heart break a little at her daughter's words. Erica rarely mentioned Eric. Her daughter had been just a baby when he'd died. Ryann kept her back to her daughter and continued stirring the soup, waiting to hear what Richard would say next.

"I'm sorry to hear that. It's hard when people we love die."

"I never knew my daddy. He died right after I was born. But I still love him. Do you think he knows that?"

Ryann caught her breath. Were these the things her daughter thought about? And why on earth was she talking like this with someone she'd just met?

"I'm sure he does. I'm betting he knows what an awesome little girl he has."

"You think so?"

"Of course."

Ryann felt a tear making its way down her cheek. She shrugged her shoulder to rub it away. Trying not to sniff, she started slathering butter on the bread to make the sandwiches.

"I think I'm going to like living here." Erica's little voice gave away nothing.

Ryann dared to take a quick glance over her shoulder to see if she could tell how Erica was doing. Instead, she caught Richard's eye. Whipping her head back around, she continued making the sandwiches. She didn't want him to know she'd been crying.

She wasn't crying over Eric. He'd been gone too long. No, she was crying because life left her to raise her daughter by herself.

Clearing her throat, she called over her shoulder, "Dinner will be ready soon. Can you test your sugar, sweetie, or do you need my help?"

"I can do it."

Ryann hoped the dim lighting hid her feelings. She wasn't ready to deal with her past. Not yet, and maybe not ever.

Richard had spent little time around children, but he liked Erica so far. She'd been very matter of fact about her father's death. He itched to know more. He wanted to know if the man's death was the reason Ryann was homeless and living in his uncle's barn.

Walking back to where Ryann stood at the stove, he asked quietly, "Can I help with anything?"

Ryann shook her head and didn't raise her eyes to him. He thought he'd caught a look of sadness when she'd glanced over her shoulder at her daughter a moment ago, but she'd turned away so fast, he wasn't sure. Maybe she still loved her husband.

Giving in to an impulse, he reached out and tipped her head up to see her face better. He saw her eyes widen in shock. He also saw the remnants of tears on her cheeks. It was obvious she still had deep feelings for her deceased husband. Maybe she wasn't over him after all.

"I'm sorry," he whispered, releasing his hold on her. He pushed his hands into his pockets so he wouldn't give into a second urge to wipe away the wetness on her cheeks.

"It's okay. She was only a baby when he died. He..." Ryann's breath hitched, "he never got to meet his daughter."

Richard wanted to ask more questions, but Ryann straightened and turned away. She busied herself with stirring the soup.

His thoughts turned to Sloane. He wondered how she would act in Ryann's situation, but he realized how implausible that would be. Sloane had never gone without anything in her life. He knew Ryann couldn't say the same.

"Can you bring this to the table?" Ryann pointed at the soup pan. "I'll grab the sandwiches."

The two soon had everything at the table. Richard pulled out a chair for Ryann. "Here. The chef should have the place of honor."

Ryann chuckled. "Reserve that thought until you've eaten it. I'm no chef, but it should be edible."

"Considering I was going to have a cold sandwich, I'm thrilled already. I make a mean peanut butter and jelly, but that's it."

"I love peanut butter and jelly!" Erica cried and clapped her hands. "What's your favorite kind of jelly?"

Richard laughed. "I've never thought about the answer to that question before."

"Get used to those types of questions. She's full of them and has a never-ending supply." Ryann smiled at her daughter.

"I love strawberry. My favorite is when Mommy makes it." Erica licked her lips. "It's so delicious! I could eat a whole jar all by myself."

"You make your own jelly?" Richard raised an eyebrow at Ryann, a thought beginning to form.

"When I have my own kitchen and the time. And I've had neither lately."

"Mommy, don't forget my shot." Erica handed the meter to her mother to show her the number. She'd tested her own sugar while the two adults had been talking.

"Right. Richard, would you mind praying? Then you can start eating while I get Erica situated."

Richard hoped he kept the surprise off his face. Pray? He couldn't remember the last time he'd prayed. Maybe when he'd been sitting at this very table with his aunt and uncle.

"Um, yeah, sure." He was glad for the low light that hopefully hid his discomfort. He quickly mumbled something he hoped would pass muster, something he remembered his uncle saying before a meal. As soon as he said "amen," he stuffed a bite of sandwich into his mouth and began to chew.

He kept his head down over his food, acting as if he was concentrating on the meal, while glancing over at Ryann and her daughter. He saw her take a vial and a syringe, add some liquid from the vial to the syringe, and then inject her daughter. Erica never made a peep.

Ryann wasn't the only strong one in that family.

"I think my favorite might be strawberry too, Erica. But I think I need some of the jelly your mom makes just to be sure."

Richard winked at the little girl. Erica giggled and began eating her dinner.

"Thank you for cooking, Ryann. I didn't mean to leave it all to you. I'm kind of capable of making food. Well, to be honest, I'm excellent at ordering food."

Erica giggled, "Ordering food isn't making food, silly."

"It is for me," Richard again winked at the little girl, who giggled at him.

He turned to Ryann to continue. "When we're done here, I'd like to give you a tour. I know it will be hard to see everything by lantern light, but it will give you an idea of the project."

Erica's head bobbed back and forth between the two adults as they talked. Her eyes widened. "Are we going to live here, Mommy?"

Richard gave Ryann a quick glance. "Did I say too much?"

"No, it's okay." Turning to her daughter, Ryann continued, "Yes, once Mr. Richard has the electricity turned back on, we're going to move in upstairs."

"Do you *have* to turn on the electricity? Laura didn't have any! Please, can't you leave it off?" Erica clasped her hands under her chin and turned her wide, pleading eyes, first to Ryann and then to Richard.

Richard shot Ryann a look while he worked to contain his laughter. It was harder to do as Ryann rolled her eyes at him before turning to answer her daughter.

"Sweetie, you may want to live like Laura, but I certainly don't. I don't have time to bash our clothing on the rocks to clean them. Or haul water. Or sweep floors. Or bake bread. Understand?"

"Okay," Erica said, sadness creeping into her voice as she lowered her hands. "I guess you're right. But do you think we could make bread? Some day? I love your homemade bread, Mommy."

Ryann chuckled. "Once we have a working oven, yes, we'll make bread."

Richard listened, more ideas beginning to form. For now, he would keep them to himself, but he was seeing a way to make this farm thing work. He just needed to figure out a way to convince Ryann to help him.

Ten

Ryann

Ryann smiled as she stretched. Sunlight was streaming through the window, warming the spot where she lay. Erica, who was snoring slightly, was curled into Ryann's side. Ryann tucked an arm around her, pulling her daughter closer. Her thoughts drifted back to the evening before.

Dinner had been, well, interesting seemed to be the right word. She liked the man she was getting to know. She was seeing glimpses of the boy she remembered. Richard had been a gentleman throughout the evening. Even when he'd found her crying while she stirred the soup.

Her stomach flipped as she remembered how he'd lifted her chin. His brown eyes had looked warm and deep in the low light of the lantern. He'd given her such a look of caring. It made her realize just how much she missed having someone around who was concerned about her. All her focus went to Erica. It was nice, for a moment, to have someone do the same for her. Something she'd missed since losing Eric.

Eric. Memories of her late husband flooded back to her. She'd kept the thoughts at bay for too long. Grief had consumed her in the beginning, and then Erica had arrived. Ryann's only thought after the birth of her daughter was survival, especially in those first few months.

She turned her head on the pillow to study her daughter, who was her greatest treasure. It had been hard to raise Erica on her own, but she never regretted having her.

Ryann let her thoughts drift back, working to pick out the memories that brought her the most joy of when she'd been with Eric.

One night at a party, Ryann had met Eric. Despite being out of high school for a couple of years, she was still living at home and taking community college classes nearby while she saved to go to Bowdoin. The more time passed, the more her dream seemed to slip further away.

It was the reason she'd let her friend talk her into going to the beach party. It was something Ryann wouldn't have done normally, but she was realizing the longer it took her to get to Bowdoin, the more likely it would never happen.

And then Eric Jordan had walked into her life.

The moment she'd laid eyes on him, Eric captivated Ryann. He was the center of attention, familiar with everyone at the party, except her. Two years her senior at 24, he was home on leave from the army.

Even now Ryann could remember how she'd blushed when she saw him standing there with his toned muscles, his short crew cut, and his laugh. Oh, how she'd loved his laugh. It was one that was full of confidence. Eric had known who he was, and it oozed from him, infecting all those around him with joy.

Ryann had known who she was when she'd been with him. And she missed that. She missed him. So much.

"Mommy, are we moving into the house today?" Erica still had her eyes closed as she mumbled the words.

As Ryann had known, getting Erica to sleep last night had been harder than normal. The little girl had been too excited about living the "Laura life," as she called it. Now that she knew they would soon move into the house, she was even more excited.

"Not today, but soon. Let's get you up and ready for school. Okay, kiddo?"

"Okay." Erica let out a yawn and stretched, finally opening her eyes.

"Mommy?"

"What sweetie?" Ryann asked as she rolled out of bed. She slept in sweatpants and a sweatshirt for an extra layer of warmth although, the nights were getting warmer. Spring was finally here.

All the same, she was almost as excited as Erica to be moving into a house. Even if it meant they would live with Richard right downstairs. She didn't want to think about the feelings that thought brought now.

"Do you miss Daddy?"

And that question stopped any thought Ryann had of what Richard might look like in the morning. She caught her breath. She hadn't realized until last night how much Erica missed her father. While she thought she'd done a good job being both mother and father to her little girl, it was obviously not enough.

"I do, honey. So much." Ryann sat back on the bed next to her daughter, reaching out to stroke her hair.

"Me too."

"I'm sorry, baby. I'm sorry your daddy isn't here with you. He would have loved you so much."

Ryann gave Erica a tight hug, holding back the tears that seemed to hover just below the surface too often of late. Taking a deep breath, she gave her daughter one last tight squeeze before releasing her.

"You know you can ask me anything you want about daddy, right? You can talk about him anytime."

"Ok, Mommy. I got to use the privy!"

Erica scrambled over Ryann, jamming her feet into a pair of bright pink Crocs. The little girl hurried from the room. Ryann held back the laughter, trying to bubble out. Erica kept adding words she learned from the Little House books to her vocabulary.

Kids were far more resilient than adults, it seemed. While she wanted to curl back up in bed and cry about all she missed about being a wife, her daughter seemed to move forward at light speed.

Ryann went to heat water for coffee and oatmeal. Last night, Richard had graciously offered to drive Erica to school and take Ryann to the garage to see about someone coming out to get her car. She hoped the issue with her car was minor. Relying on Richard too much too soon went against her nature. She valued the independence of having her own vehicle too much to give it up easily.

She had today off from the café, and it looked like she was going to spend most of it with Richard. Her stomach gave a little flip at his name, but she shoved the feeling down. She needed to keep this professional. This Richard wasn't the same as her childhood friend. He'd grown up and so had she. They'd changed, and she needed to remember that.

Ryann stood in the middle of the living room, making notes on what needed to be done. Every room she'd examined closer since getting back from town was so full of stuff. She'd known the house had seemed packed last night when Richard had given her a tour, but the lantern light had hidden the corners.

Richard was outside checking on the trees while Ryann worked in here. If the outside looked anything like it did in the house, they had their work cut out for them.

Everything was neatly in place inside, but there was just so much of it. Every cabinet she'd opened had been so full, she didn't think a beetle would have fit. Each closet was the same. Every available spot that could hold something did so, and then some. She wasn't sure how she would ever get it all sorted before the end of the year, let alone the end of the summer. She wondered how Richard would feel about renting a dumpster and just tossing everything.

"Do you want to see the upstairs again?"

Ryann jumped as she turned to see Richard standing behind her. She swatted at his arm with her notebook. "You scared me! I didn't hear you come in."

Smiling, Richard dodged the blow. "Sorry. I thought you might want to tackle upstairs first so you and Erica can move in. Plus, there isn't as much up there. At least it didn't look like it."

Ryann started towards the stairs. "Sure, let's go."

Not waiting for an answer, she headed up the narrow staircase at the front of the house. She heard Richard as he hurried across the room to join her.

Ryann glanced back at him as she neared the top of the stairs. "When is your deadline again? Because I don't know how we're going to get this all done. There's *a lot* of stuff here."

As she went to take the last step up, her foot tangled in the floor runner. She lost her balance and felt herself falling backward. "Oh!" She scrambled to grab the banister. Suddenly, a pair of powerful hands gripped her waist.

"Hold on. I've got you."

She clutched the banister with one hand and the other found its way to one of Richard's on her waist. "Thanks," she breathed out, working to slow her racing heart. She told herself her heart was beating fast because of the adrenaline and not because Richard had caught her.

"My pleasure."

Ryann wanted to stay where she was, held up by this strong man, but she took a quick step forward. She was heading into dangerous territory and needed to regroup. Her focus needed to be Erica, not having a man in her life.

It was the reason she'd never dated after losing Eric. While she yearned to have someone to share life with, she wouldn't date until her daughter was older. She'd vowed to herself not to bring different men into her daughter's life, only to have them leave when things didn't work out between them. She didn't want that for her daughter.

No, she wanted a man who would stay.

"Hey, I was wondering if I could add on to our agreement?" Richard asked.

Ryann felt her face flush at his gaze. She needed to remember this was Richard, not Ricky. Maybe this was a bad idea. If he had this much effect on her now, what would it be like by the time they finished renovating the house?

"I'll leave today." Ryann made to move past him.

Richard held up his hands. "Hear me out."

"No, you hear *me* out." Ryann poked a finger into his chest and tried not to think about how solid it felt. "The agreement was for me to help you hoe this place out. No more. No less. I'm not that kind of girl. Seriously." Ryann felt her anger growing. So much for thinking she knew this man since they had a shared past.

"Ryann! I want you to cook. That's it!" Richard called after her as she started down the stairs. "What kind of man do you take me for anyway?"

She stopped mid-stride, halfway down the stairs. "Cook? You want me to cook?" Ryann looked back up at him in confusion.

"I'm just asking if you'll be willing to do some cooking in addition to the rest. It doesn't have to be every night, but I'm hoping when you're here, you'll take pity on me and make food.

I really am hopeless in the kitchen. Maybe you could even teach me some basics?"

"Oh." Ryann slowly walked back upstairs, careful not to trip again since Richard wasn't behind her. She'd overreacted. Great. "Yeah. I could do that. Sure."

Taking a deep breath, she let it out slowly along with the anger. *Great, now he's really going to think I'm a nut job.* "Um, sorry."

"I want you to know I would never take advantage of you, Ryann."

She glanced up at him and saw the sincerity in his eyes. Nodding her head, she turned and started down the hallway. Maybe it was time for her to learn to trust again.

Eleven

Richard

Richard trailed after Ryann as they headed down the upstairs hallway towards the front bedroom. He tried to forget how good it had felt to hold her, even for just a moment.

It had been weird being around Ryann. On one hand, he felt like he knew her. But on the other, so many years had passed that they acted like strangers. Memories of the time they'd spent together kept popping up, but life had continued. It didn't matter what their past had been like.

Maybe it would be better to just take some time to focus on the farm rather than a relationship. He needed some time to figure out what he really wanted, what mattered to him. He didn't have time for someone in his life anyway, and especially not a woman with a child.

Although Erica was adorable. And that was a lot coming from him. He smiled as he remembered the rapid-fire questions from last night. Not only had she quizzed him about his favorite kind of jelly, but she'd forced him to consider what his favorite animal was, his favorite tree, and his favorite book. He'd tried to appear as if he'd known the answer to each, but he'd just picked the first thing that came to mind. Bear. Maple. *The Woodbender*.

"How good are you at making bread and the other stuff Erica mentioned last night?" Richard let the question slip out before he could stop himself.

"Pretty good. Why?" Ryann entered the first bedroom at the top of the stairs. Richard trailed after her.

"Just an idea I'm working on. Have you ever sold anything you've made?"

Ryann didn't even twitch at the rapidness of his speech. Erica must have gotten her used to it, and Richard was having a hard time controlling his ideas. They were crashing around his skull like a ping-pong ball.

"Sold it? Sometimes. I make it as gifts and to swap for things we might need if I don't have cash." Ryann's cheeks reddened. "And sometimes I help Brenda at the café if she needs a day off."

Richard thought she looked adorable when she blushed like that. And while he wanted to explore the idea of selling things like jelly and homemade bread at the farm, he also didn't want to spook Ryann again. He kept to his original idea. "Do you think there would be a good market here for things like that? Like a farm store? And not seasonally, but year-round?"

"Maybe. The Haven Farmer's Market always seems to do well in the summer. I sometimes set up a booth there, and I'm usually sold out long before it's time to pack up. People seem to like that sort of thing, especially the tourists. What were you thinking of doing?"

"Maybe nothing. I love the idea of getting the apple farm up and running again, but it's only one thing. What if I could bring in other people, people like you, and create a cooperative store? One where people could come in and sell their items in one place, year-round. It was just something that sparked to life last night when Erica mentioned your jam and bread."

Richard trailed off. He knew he could spend hours talking about the idea. It was how he processed things. And it was one thing Sloane had always disliked.

"It might work. I think you'll need to figure out how you'd stock things. Would people sell on commission, or would you buy products outright and resell them? There are pros and cons to each method."

"I agree. It's a lot to consider, but first we need to figure out what to do with the house." Bringing the conversation back to what they were supposed to be focused on, Richard asked, "What do you think of this room?"

They were standing in what his uncle had always called the "front bedroom." It had the best view of the dooryard outside. There was only a double bed, covered in a handmade quilt, and a dresser against one wall. A small rag rug in colors matching the quilt lay on the floor beside the bed. Of course, there was a small bookcase overflowing with dusty volumes. Other than a small bedside table with a lamp on it, the room was empty.

Richard crossed to the opposite side, pulling open the closet door. Ahhhh, that's where it all was. The closet was full of boxes. There wasn't an inch of space for anything else.

He coughed and shut the door, dust filling the air.

"Found it," he choked out.

"Found what?" Ryann asked as she waved her hands in front of her face.

"The clutter. My uncle held on to everything. I'm sure those boxes contain National Geographic or Popular Mechanics issues. Something he was sure he'd need 'someday.'" Richard laughed as he made finger quotes around the last word.

Ryann turned in a slow circle in the middle of the room. "Erica could have this room. The only thing it needs is a thorough cleaning. And the bedding just needs to be washed."

She raised an eyebrow at him. "And I'm not going to the river to wash it either."

Richard laughed. "No, I wouldn't dare ask that of you. The electricity gets connected tomorrow. If there isn't a working washer and dryer, I'll get one hooked up soon. Is there a laundromat around somewhere until we get that sorted out?"

"There is. Once my car is fixed, I can do laundry and groceries on my day off."

"I'm not asking you to do all that. But you'll need to get things washed to move in, so let me know, and I'll make sure you have the money needed to do that."

"I can afford to wash our bedding and clothing, Ricky!"

Richard watched as color once more started at the base of Ryann's neck and flooded her face.

"I haven't heard that name in a long time." Richard bunched his hands and shoved them in his pockets. He would spook Ryann if he touched her. And if he were honest, he wanted to do more than just stroke her face. He wanted to pull her close and kiss her. Thoroughly. He needed to get himself under control.

So much for swearing off women for a while. But there was something about Ryann that just felt... well, felt right.

"Sorry, I didn't mean. I... well..." Ryann wiped her hands on her jeans. "What do you prefer to be called?"

Richard cleared his throat, not wanting to let the moment become more awkward. "Either works. It's just that no one's called me Ricky in years.

Changing the subject, Richard said, "C'mon, I'll show you the other two bedrooms and the bathroom." He walked out of the room and took a left down the hallway. He didn't mind that Ryann had called him by his childhood nickname. In fact, hearing it again made him realize how much he missed hearing it. Especially from her.

He'd adopted the use of his full name when he entered college. He'd wanted to shake off the past and start fresh. But maybe forgetting the past wasn't what he needed to do. Maybe he needed to remember the good things from before and see how it fit with his future. Like the woman in front of him. She could be a bridge between the two. He liked that idea.

He opened the door to the bathroom. He remembered the summer he'd helped Uncle Art build it. What had once been a fourth bedroom was now a spacious bathroom. Simple enough with a vanity, double sink, a tub with a shower enclosure, and a toilet. They'd left the closet, so there was a place to store linens.

Opening it, he expected to see more boxes. Surprised, he found there were still towels and sheets filling the shelves.

Suddenly, he jumped back with a short yell. A small streak of gray raced across the floor and out the open door.

Ryann shrieked and jumped practically straight up. Her head swiveled, looking for a place to land. She ran for the tub and hopped in before Richard could catch his breath.

"Was that... was that... what was that?" Ryann got out between panicked breaths.

"A mouse. It was just a mouse. I think we may have scared it more than it scared us." Richard chuckled as his pulse slowed.

"I doubt that." Ryann continued to scan the floor. "Where did it go? Do you see it anywhere?"

"It ran out the door. I'm sure it's found a new hiding place. It's safe to come out." Richard reached out a hand to Ryann to help her over the edge of the tub.

Ryann stared at his hand and then up at his face. "If you think I'm getting out of here, you're crazy."

"It's safe. I promise. It's long gone."

"Improbable."

"Ryann." Richard couldn't help it. He laughed. "That mouse was way more scared of us. We're giants in its eyes. C'mon," he gestured for her to step out of the tub. "I'll pick up some traps. And now that there are people living here again, it'll find a new home."

Ryann still hesitated before taking a slow step out of the tub. "If that thing runs across my foot, I'm going to slap you."

She raised an eyebrow at him, and Richard laughed again. Stretching out a hand to her, his heart bumped out an extra rhythm when she took it. "I'll protect you," he said as he squeezed her hand.

Then he couldn't help but tease her just a little. "You know mice can jump, right? That tub wouldn't have stopped it."

Richard worked hard not to laugh again as Ryann shuddered.

"I hate mice. Their little beady eyes and their little feet. So gross."

"C'mon. Just be glad it wasn't a snake."

Richard let his laugh ring out as Ryann's eyes widened. He managed to ask between laughter, "Where did the little girl who used to throw snakes at me go?"

"She grew up."

Still holding her hand, he tugged her forward. "Let's go check out the other two bedrooms."

He squeezed her hand once more before letting it go with reluctance. Richard tried to keep his mind focused on what they were doing up here. He should make notes about anything they'd need to make the place livable, not be thinking about the gorgeous woman standing beside him.

Except all he could focus on was how her hand had felt in his. Maybe too much. After all, it had only been a few weeks since he'd tried to propose to Sloane. He shouldn't be having feelings for someone else this quickly.

But if he were being honest with himself, he knew what he'd had with Sloane had been more about his career than his love life. And he didn't like what that said about him. Not at all.

He followed Ryann as she walked out of the bathroom and headed to the next bedroom. His mind still worked on processing what his next move should be—not only with the house, but with Ryann.

The second bedroom was like the first. There was only a bed, a small side table and lamp, and a dresser. Once again, the closet was full of boxes, but the bedroom floor was clear. A quick clean would make it livable.

"This will work for me. That way I'll be close to Erica in the night. There's one more bedroom, right?" Ryann turned and walked out the door, not waiting for an answer.

Once more, Richard trailed after her. They soon stood in front of the door leading into the last bedroom. This was the room that had been his whenever he'd stayed at the farm. He wondered what it looked like now after all these years.

"If you use those two as bedrooms, you could set this up as a living room. It should be big enough for a couch and a TV." Richard tried to push the door open so they could go inside. The door moved an inch before stopping.

"What is it? Is the door stuck?" Ryann asked as she tried to peer over his shoulder.

Richard put his shoulder against the door and shoved. There was a scraping sound, and the door gave way a few more inches, allowing them to see inside.

He stepped back, mouth hanging open. Inside the room were boxes filling the space from floor to ceiling. They were all neatly stacked, but there was a solid wall of boxes staring him in the face. How his aunt and uncle had even gotten the last few boxes in there and shut the door, he had no idea.

"Wow!" Ryann squeezed past him and tried to fit through the doorway. She pushed her head inside but couldn't move any further forward. "How are we going to get inside?"

"I think I can take the door off the hinges." Richard ran a hand through his hair and turned to Ryann. "How much do you need a living room right away?"

She laughed. "Not that much. We'll survive with just the two bedrooms for now. What are you going to do with all that stuff?"

"One word. Dumpster."

Twelve

R yann drummed her fingers on the steering wheel of the borrowed car as she waited for Erica to get out of school. It had been a busy day all ready.

She'd spent the morning cleaning the two bedrooms upstairs so they could move out of the barn tonight. Ryann thought she might be even more excited than Erica about the new sleeping location. While she loved her daughter, she was looking forward to having her own bed. And, honestly, she couldn't wait to have her own room again. Sharing the small barn room with her daughter for the last few weeks had been tough.

Stretching her arms, she let her head fall against the back of the seat and closed her eyes. Ryann couldn't believe she'd called Richard Ricky this morning. The nickname had slipped out.

And freaking out over the mouse. She groaned at the memory. But she'd clung to his hand like the nasty little thing was going to jump out at her any moment and claw at her eyes. She shuddered. She hated rodents.

After she'd finished cleaning the rooms, she'd stripped the beds. The clutter in the closets and the third room would have to wait for another day.

Richard had disappeared outside after the mouse incident, leaving Ryann alone to work. He'd given her permission to borrow his car to take all the bedding to be washed. While in town, she'd picked up more cleaning supplies and some groceries.

"Hi, Mommy!"

Ryann's eyes opened at the sound of her daughter's voice. Erica climbed into the back seat and clipped her seatbelt. "Ready!"

Heading back to the farm, Ryann tried to keep an ear tuned to her daughter's chatter about her day, but found her thoughts floating back to Richard. She kept wondering what it would have been like if he'd held her instead of just her hand. No one had hugged her, other than her daughter, in far too long.

"And then Remy told me I needed to be quiet. Like he ever stops talking! Mom, are we homeless?"

"What?" Ryann's thoughts slammed back to the present. "Who said that?"

"Remy's mom told him we were homeless. Are we?"

"No, baby. We're not homeless." She reached a hand over the seat and Erica grasped it. Ryann squeezed once before releasing it. Dread filled her at the sound of the word "homeless" and the connotation it brought. It wasn't like they were living on the streets. They had a roof over their heads—even if it was a barn roof for a few weeks.

Maybe she should call and have a little chat with Sarah, Remy's mom. Not that it would do much good. Sarah was the biggest gossip in town. All it would do would give her reason to spread more tales. The woman seemed to thrive on drama.

Changing the subject, Ryann said, "I'm going to need your help to get the beds made and our things moved. Are you up for that?"

"Yeah! I can't wait to live in the farmhouse! Do you think Laura's house was just like it? I bet it was! I bet Laura had a bedroom just like mine."

Ryann laughed before answering her daughter. She was thankful her daughter was still easily distractible. "I doubt Laura had a house like this one, honey. For one thing, Laura wouldn't have had electricity." Well, technically neither did they yet, but Ryann was hoping it was on soon.

"Well, I'm still going to pretend!" Erica turned to look out the window, humming under her breath.

Before she'd picked up Erica, Ryann had swung by the garage to check on her car. The Ritz brothers who owned it had diagnosed the issue as a busted fuel pump. They'd assured her it was easily fixable, and it would be ready for her tomorrow. She was thankful the issue hadn't been worse.

Pulling into the farm, Ryann parked the car near the porch. "All right, help me unload everything, kiddo."

Erica slung her backpack on and grabbed a bag of groceries, skipping into the house.

Ryann hoisted the laundry basket full of clean bedding on one hip and grabbed a bag of groceries with her other hand. She carefully navigated up the rickety steps to the porch. Thankfully, Erica had left the door ajar. Giving it a push with her hip, she headed inside.

Stepping over the backpack her daughter had dropped on the floor, Ryann set the laundry basket on the couch. Bending, she snagged the bag of groceries Erica had left in the middle of the floor and carried both bags to the kitchen. Her daughter had disappeared in the few minutes it had taken her to walk inside.

Sighing, as she set the groceries on the counter, Ryann took a moment to realize how blessed she was to be here. God was looking out for them–even if it wasn't in the exact way Ryann would have wanted. God had blessed her. She knew this. There was no other answer.

"Thank you," she whispered, closing her eyes and continuing her prayer in her head. "Amen. Now get to work," she said out loud. She laughed. If Richard heard her talking to herself like this, he'd think she was crazy and kick her out. No, Richard was a good man. She was beginning to see that.

Why else would he have let a woman he barely remembered from his past stay with him? A woman with a young daughter, no less. He could have kicked her out of the barn the moment he'd found them. Instead, he'd been working to help her.

Turning to go back for the rest of the groceries, she jumped. Richard was standing in the doorway, covered in dirt, smiling his devastatingly handsome smile at her.

"Oh!" Her hand flew to her chest. "You need to stop doing that!" She let out a shaky laugh as she took a couple of deep breaths to get her racing heart to slow.

"Do you always talk to yourself?" He raised an eyebrow at her as he walked to the sink. There was a jug of water there with soap, and he began to wash.

"Only when I think I'm alone. Why are you so dirty?"

"I'm working on getting the orchard cleared. There are a lot of downed branches. Think Erica would want to help me?

"Maybe. If you tell her Laura Ingalls did work like that, she'll jump at the chance."

"Laura?" Erica popped into the kitchen. "What did Laura do?"

"See!" Ryann laughed at her daughter's timing. "Where did you go? Never mind, Richard wants to know if you would like to help him work in the orchard."

"Yeah!" Erica danced around the kitchen. "Let's go!"

Placing a hand on her daughter's shoulder to get her attention, Ryann said, "Not so fast, little one. You need a snack first. Let's get your blood sugar up a little before you go haul branches."

Ryann went over to the bags of groceries she'd already brought in and took out a package of peanut butter crackers. "Here, you're favorite." She handed them to her daughter, along with a bottle of water. "Eat up and then you can go help."

While her daughter sat down to eat, Ryann asked Richard, "Will you help me bring in the rest of the stuff from the car?"

"Sure." He followed her out of the house.

As they headed down the steps, Ryann said, "You need to keep a close eye on Erica while you're out in the orchard. I'll send more snacks. If she gets cranky with you, make her test her blood sugar. She knows how. If it's anywhere in the 70s or lower, give her a snack."

Ryann was going to have to trust Richard with her daughter's health. She needed to make sure he understood the importance of monitoring Erica. Things could change quickly, and if he wasn't paying attention, it could be disastrous.

"Sure, I can do that."

He didn't seem phased by the prospect of taking Erica with him. Ryann wrestled with the idea more before saying, "Maybe I should go with you."

"Ryann, you can trust me. I'll make sure she's okay."

"I'm just a phone call away. Just... well, just be careful, okay?" Ryann handed him four of the remaining bags and took the last two before slamming the trunk closed.

Changing the topic, Ryann said, "My car will be ready tomorrow. Can you bring me into town to pick it up?"

"Sure. And I wanted to let you know I called the electric company. They assured me we have power, so I doubled checked the panel. There seems to be a short somewhere and I can't figure it out. An electrician will be out tomorrow. I also have a plumber coming to give me a quote on updating the bathrooms and kitchen to something more this century."

"That will make Erica unhappy. She's loved living in the past here. However, I will be happy to have a hot shower." Ryann looked forward to not having to heat water to sponge off or use baby wipes to clean up.

Richard laughed as he turned to bring the bags inside. "I just wish my list of things to fix was getting shorter and not longer."

Ryann followed him. What he was taking on here was huge, and getting the house updated was only the beginning. She didn't even know what needed to be done in the orchard to get that producing again.

Dumping the bags on the counter, Ryann laughed at her daughter. While they'd been outside, Erica had finished her snack. She was hopping from one foot to the other while chanting, "Let's go! Let's go! Let's go!"

Richard rumpled Erica's hair and laughed. "Give your mom a minute to get things ready and, then we'll go work."

Ryann quickly added some juice boxes and fruit snacks to her daughter's backpack. All the while working to keep her heart from swelling with emotion at how Richard treated her daughter. He didn't act like she was fragile. He seemed to enjoy having her with him, otherwise why would he have invited her to go help him in the orchard?

It felt, well, it felt like what things might have been like if Eric had lived. A complete family. Swallowing hard to stem her rising emotions, Ryann handed the backpack to Erica. "Keep this with you, honey. Test your sugar in about an hour, okay? Be safe and listen to Mr. Richard."

"Okay, Mommy! Bye!" And with that Ryann watched her daughter skip out of the house, holding Richard's hand.

Richard tossed a dazzling smile over his shoulder before they both disappeared out the door. Ryann found herself alone in the house.

She shook her head at herself. She was being ridiculous if she thought Richard would want to get involved with someone like her, no matter how he seemed to feel about Erica. What man wanted to start a relationship with a single mom with a seven-year-old who asked a million questions? What kind of man would want an instant family like that?

Turning, she leaned against the counter and let out a shaky laugh. She was in so much trouble because there was a kernel of hope growing inside her that was hoping Richard was *exactly* that kind of man. He was worming his way into her heart, just like he'd once done all those years ago.

Thirteen

Richard

R ichard stared at the estimate from the plumber and tried not to groan. He loved his Uncle Art, but the man had updated nothing at the farmhouse in decades. Just about every faucet leaked, and the toilets cracked. All of it needed to be replaced. There was water pooling in the basement from leaking throughout the pipes in the house. If Richard ever had any hope of selling the property, he would need to update all the plumbing fixtures and make sure all the lines were solid.

Thankfully, the electrician had at least fixed the power easily. A breaker had popped at some point, probably from a storm. Once Richard had discovered the issue, he'd tried resetting it himself before giving up and calling in the electrician.

The man had raised an eyebrow at the panel, however, and strongly suggested Richard update the electrical. That estimate was on its way as well. Richard wasn't sure he wanted it.

The cost of inheriting Saltwater Orchard was starting to worry him. Money wasn't an issue. After paying off his student loans, he'd worked hard to build his savings and investment accounts. A year off from his bank job shouldn't hurt him too much.

However, he needed to make the farm viable. Otherwise, what was the point? If he couldn't make the farm work, he might as well take anything with sentimental value and give the rest to the Haven Fire Department.

He'd known this project wouldn't be easy, but it was for that reason he'd wanted to do it. Richard loved a good challenge. He wanted something that would be interesting and diverse and hard work. Banking had lost its luster in recent years, which was something he hadn't realized until he'd arrived at the farm.

He no longer woke up dreading his day. In fact, it was quite the opposite. He woke up looking forward to what the day would bring. Ryann's face popped into his head. It wasn't just because of the pretty brunette that was now living on his second floor. At least not the entire reason.

Richard stood in the doorway to the den, hands on hips as he surveyed the room. He let out a loud sigh. There were books everywhere. Three sides of the room had floor to ceiling bookshelves. Each shelf had books crammed into every available spot. There had to be thousands of books here.

He gave in and let out a loud groan. "What am I going to do with all of this?" he muttered under his breath.

"Now who's talking to themselves?"

Startled, he spun and saw Ryann walking down the stairs. She was so beautiful. Her hair was in her customary high ponytail. She was already dressed for work in a pair of black pants and a white blouse. She had her hands behind her back as she finished tying on her red apron.

"Richard? Are you okay?"

He blinked. Ryann stood in front of him, face tipped up to catch his gaze, frowning at him. He shook his head and smiled down at her.

"Sorry, yeah. I just got lost in thought there for a minute."

With her hair up, all he could do was stare at her neck and that little spot where it met her shoulder. He leaned forward because the thought of planting a kiss right there was almost more than he could resist.

Shaking his head slightly, he took a hasty step back before he acted on his thoughts. *Get a grip, Mosely!*

He cleared his throat before saying out loud, "I was just wondering what to do with all these books. What do you think?" Richard turned, making himself wait for her to answer.

"Do you want to keep them?"

"Not particularly. I like to read, but not enough to have my own library."

"There's an idea." Ryann tapped a finger on her chin.

"I just said I didn't want my own library."

"I heard you. Not you. The town library. Every spring, they do a massive book sale to raise funds to buy new books."

"Um, doesn't that defeat the purpose? They *have* books already. Why sell them to buy more? Why not just keep what they have?"

"The library can't keep every single book it's ever owned. There's just not enough room. Well, they'd look like this." Ryann waved a hand at the room. "Once people stop checking out a book, the library sells it. They only keep books on the shelves that people borrow."

"Huh, I never thought of that. Makes sense." Richard put his hands on his hips and looked around the room once more. "Do you think they'd take *all* of them? There's got to be hundreds in here."

"I'll stop by and ask while I'm in town today." Turning, Ryann yelled up the stairs, "Put the book down and let's go, Erica!"

Shaking her head, she turned back to Richard. "She's a little put out you had the electricity fixed."

Richard chuckled. "I can't say the same for myself. It's kind of nice to flip a switch at night and have lights."

"Agreed," Ryann said as she laughed with him.

The clattering of feet announced Erica's arrival. "Hi, Mr. Richard! Bye, Mr. Richard!"

Richard laughed outright as the little girl flew by him out the front door.

"If only I had that much energy," Ryann muttered as she hurried after her daughter. She waved a hand over her shoulder at Richard as she practically ran out the door after Erica.

Richard wasn't sure what he would do when the house was done. He enjoyed having Ryann and her daughter in the house. Far too much.

Richard let loose with a loud "Achoo!" as the dust from the books billowed up around him. He had been sneezing all morning as he stacked books into boxes. How his uncle had the time to read so many, he didn't know. Then again, the man was retired. Maybe that was the key.

He had two entire bookcases emptied, and the room was starting to echo slightly. Standing, he leaned back to stretch out his back before walking over to the next case to unload it.

Starting at the top, he reached up and pulled a stack of books off. An envelope floated down, landing at his feet. Setting the books on a nearby chair, he stooped to pick it up.

The front had the words "The Truth" scrawled across it. He didn't recognize the handwriting. Flipping it over, he opened the flap and pulled out a single piece of paper. Unfolding it, he began reading.

The Truth

Life is messy.
Life is hard.
But without You by my side, it would be impossible to bear.
Thank You for always being there.

Life with You is still messy.
Life with You is still hard.
Your grace is a lifeline when I stumble and fall.
Your Word always guides me through it all.

Life will always be messy.
Life will always be hard.
But Your truth is the rock on which I stand.
For You always answer all of life's demands.

Matthew 19:25-26

Richard read the words again. He knew the reference at the bottom had something to do with the Bible. Scanning the books still on the cases, he spotted a thick, black book on a shelf nearby.

Pulling it off the shelf, he sat in his uncle's recliner. He let out a small groan at sitting down for a few minutes. Letting the Bible fall open, he began looking for the book of Matthew. It took him a few minutes, but he got there. Flipping the pages, he found the verses referenced in the poem.

He read them once, twice, and then moved to the start of the chapter. Settling back into the chair, he continued reading. He forgot time as the truth of the words began to sink into his soul.

Fourteen

Ryann

"O uch!" Ryann yelled as she pinched her finger between the box she carried, and the side of the truck Richard had rented to haul off the books. She dropped the box onto the tailgate. Richard would have to lift it into place. She gave a grateful sigh and shook her hand to help get rid of the pain. This was the last load of books being donated.

Richard had spent the day packing up the books. She'd already worked the morning shift at the café. And now she'd spent the afternoon helping to load and haul the books to the library. She was looking forward to getting off her feet.

It surprised Ryann at how many trips they'd made so far. The donation of books had thrilled the head librarian. Since there were so many, they'd decided to hold a special "Art Carruthers Memorial Book Sale" before the annual spring festival. They also planned to do a small dedication to their historical fiction section in his name.

Glancing over at Richard as he heaved the last box over the side of the truck, Ryann swallowed hard. She was trying not to admire the biceps she could see bulging from under his sleeves. She needed to remember this was a professional relationship only. No muscle admiring allowed.

"Phew! I think I got my workout moving all these boxes. How many books do you think there were? I didn't remember to count them." Richard wiped a hand over his face, leaving behind a streak of dust on his cheek.

Ryann clenched her hands so she wouldn't reach out and wipe it off. She made herself look away before saying, "There had to be at least two thousand. Although right now it feels like two million. So many boxes! I'm not sure the library really knew what they were agreeing to."

She laughed, and Richard joined in. The work had been hard, but the house was starting to feel empty. Ryann was looking forward to ripping off the hideous wallpaper from the 1970s that covered every wall.

Erica bounced up beside Richard and tried to peer over the side. "Wow! Look at all the books! What are you going to put in that room now, Mr. Richard?"

"I'm not sure. What do you think I should do?" Richard grinned at the little girl.

His patience with her daughter as she peppered him with questions still amazed Ryann. He gave her thoughtful answers and never brushed her off. Erica seemed to always seek him out.

Ryann's head snapped up from her musings when she heard Erica squeal. Richard was holding the little girl up so she could see inside the back of the truck.

"Mr. Richard! I'm up so high!"

The delight in Ryann's heart at the sight of her daughter happy and smiling filled the empty places she hadn't even realized were in her soul. The last seven years of raising Erica by herself had been more difficult than she'd realized.

Add Erica's diabetes, and the difficult was even more challenging. Everything was just so *hard* lately.

Straightening her spine, she firmed her resolve. This was only a temporary situation. Soon enough, she'd be back on her own. She didn't want to get used to relying on someone else for help.

While it had been nice having Richard here, it wouldn't last. He'd already made that clear. It was time to stop having her little pity party. Ryann had managed to this point by herself. She could manage going forward.

"Okay, enough fooling around," Ryann said. "Let's get these books delivered. One room down. How many more to go?"

"Six, I think. And who knows how many closets." Richard set the little girl back down and tousled her hair.

Erica grinned at him. Ryann's heart clenched at the sight. Anyone watching would realize the young girl was becoming attached to Richard. Ryann would need to have a talk with Erica tonight. She didn't want her little girl's heart to be broken when they moved on.

And they would have to move on. Richard planned to fix the house, get the farm operating at a profit, and then sell it. Ryann wished she had a way to buy it, but she knew that was just a dream. One that would never come true. Just like all the rest of her dreams. She didn't even have enough money to have a place for them to live, let alone purchase a place like this.

"Are you coming?"

Ryann jumped. Richard stood holding open the truck's passenger door for her.

"Oh, yeah, sorry, I was woolgathering apparently."

"Where? I don't see any wool, Mommy."

Erica scrambled in the open door and settled herself in the middle of the bench seat.

"It's just a saying, kiddo. It means I was daydreaming." Ryann stepped onto the running board and slid onto the bench seat beside her daughter. Richard gave the door a tap before shutting it. Ryann couldn't help but watch as he hurried around to the other side.

He looked good in the black and white flannel hanging open over the white t-shirt. It was then she realized how Richard no longer looked out of place in his clothes. They fit him. He fit into Haven now.

Ryann wondered what it would feel like to run her fingers through his hair as he held her close and kissed her. She sat bolt upright.

"What's wrong, Mommy?"

"Nothing, baby." Ryann patted her daughter's knee. She shouldn't be thinking about kissing Richard or running her fingers through his hair.

That was it. Richard's hair. He'd stopped mashing it to his head with gel every day.

She glanced over to where he now sat behind the wheel. She liked how his hair covered his forehead and ears. It was messy, but in a good way. Like he had just run his hands through it. Her fingers itched to reach over and play with it where it touched the back of his neck.

Ryann stared straight ahead as she swallowed against the sudden dryness in her mouth. Because the man looked *good*. Too good. She could feel the heat creeping up her cheeks.

"Mommy, you're all red. What's wrong?"

"Nothing, baby," Ryann mumbled again, turning her head to look out the window. She couldn't meet Richard's gaze right now. Would not. Yet she glanced over at him all the same.

He was looking straight ahead with a smile on his face.

Great, just great.

I'm tired. Can I go read?" Erica whined at Ryann.

"Sure, kiddo."

Ryann watched as her daughter, with more energy than she'd shown in the last two hours, scampered off to dive into her latest book. They'd picked up the last two in the Little House series from the library when they'd dropped off the last load of books.

Ryann yawned and stretched her arms. It had been a long day of working at the café and then helping to move all the boxes of books. She would love to go curl up and read with Erica, but she needed to make supper.

She walked into the kitchen and stopped short. Richard sat at the table with his head bent over whatever he was working on. The butterflies that came to life in her stomach made her catch her breath. Richard glanced up and their eyes caught. Ryann tried to swallow, but there was nothing there. Her mouth had gone dry.

What was wrong with her? She was a grown woman, with a child, no less! She didn't have time to act like a lovestruck teenager around this man.

Turning abruptly, she began pulling ingredients out of the fridge, tossing them on the counter.

"What are you making for dinner?"

"What?" Ryann glanced at Richard with confusion.

"I asked you what you're making?"

"I heard you the first time." Flustered, Ryann turned back to the counter, trying to ignore the rumble of laughter coming from the direction of the table.

She looked at the jumble of ingredients sitting there. Ryann didn't know what to make. She'd just started grabbing ingredients since she'd been focused on something else. Well, someone else.

There was half a rotisserie chicken, bacon, lettuce, tomatoes, and pickles. Pickles? She hated pickles.

"I'm making BLTC sandwiches." That sounded as good as anything else, and she was sure there was still some potato salad. She opened the fridge door again. Sure enough, a half full container sat on the shelf. She snatched it out and added it to the pile of ingredients. She put the pickles back in before shutting the door.

"BLTC sandwiches?"

Ryann started as Richard's voice came from right behind her. She'd been concentrating so hard on what to make with the jumble of ingredients, she hadn't heard him get up and move closer.

"Bacon, lettuce, tomato, and chicken." Turning, she found him standing far closer than she'd realized. She prayed her face wouldn't heat up and give her away. She tried to back up, but found herself up against the counter.

"Um..." Ryann's voice trailed off. Looking up into Richard's eyes was a mistake. She couldn't focus on anything else but the deep brown color that seemed to pull her in. The butterflies from earlier seemed to have multiplied, causing a frenzy of dancing sensations. She swallowed against the dryness that seemed to fill her mouth again.

"Thank you for making supper for me." His voice was low and husky.

"What? Oh, of course." Ryann went to move past him, to get out of the spell of his eyes, but Richard placed a hand on her arm.

"Richard, I need to go check on Erica." But Ryann didn't move. She could barely breathe, and she knew she was blushing harder every second she stood there.

"She's fine. She has a new book. Stay. Just for a minute. I want to ask you something."

"Oh?" Ryann looked up again. She needed to get a grip on herself. Every time she made eye contact with Richard, she couldn't think of anything, not even her own name.

"I know you wanted to keep this a professional relationship, but I was wondering..."

"Mommy!"

Ryann closed her eyes at the sound of her daughter's voice ringing out from the top of the stairs.

"Be right there!" Ryann called back. "I need to go."

Richard caught her gaze and opened his mouth as if to speak, but closed it. He dropped his hand and stepped back. Ryann scurried past. She glanced back at him as she left the room. He was still standing there, watching her go.

Erica either had great timing or horrible. Ryann wasn't sure which.

Fifteen

Richard

C hurch had not been on Richard's to-do list this morning. He'd watched Ryann and Erica leave every Sunday, but he'd never felt the desire to join them. When Erica had skipped into the kitchen this morning and asked him to go, he'd surprised even himself when he'd agreed.

Shifting in the hard wooden pew, Richard glanced around to see if he knew anyone. His aunt and uncle had brought him to Seaside Chapel during his summers with them. It was the only time he'd attended church. His parents had little faith, so sleeping in on Sundays was the norm. Unlike his aunt and uncle, who had gone every Sunday morning, Sunday night, and Wednesday evening.

The pastor differed from the one Richard remembered. He recalled an older man with white hair, who had delivered his sermons in a booming baritone voice. The man now in the pulpit was younger, not much older than Richard. He had a steady voice, but it wasn't as deep as the previous pastor. But this new pastor delivered his sermon in a way that made him seem more approachable.

Richard was having a hard time paying attention to what the pastor was saying. Not because he wasn't interested, but because Ryann was sitting so close to him. It was distracting. He'd tried to leave plenty of space between the two of them when he sat down, but then one of Erica's friends had wanted to sit with her. Suddenly, he'd found his hip and thigh pressed up against Ryann's in order to make room.

Richard shifted again, trying to gain some space between him and the gorgeous distraction sitting beside him. Ryann leaned into him. Richard did his best to hold still.

"Are you okay?" The soft whisper of words tickled his ear.

Turning his head a fraction of an inch, he leaned close, inhaling the scent that screamed Ryann to him. Vanilla and outdoors and coffee. He stopped himself from leaning in further and whispered back, "Yeah, no problem."

A throat cleared behind them and he straightened, glancing at Ryann, an apology forming on his lips. She patted his knee as she mouthed, "It's okay."

He instantly recalled a time when he'd sat with Ryann, just like this, during a church service when they had been much younger. And his aunt had nearly boxed his ears for all the whispering back and forth the two of them had done. His aunt never allowed them to sit together after that.

As he worked to focus his mind on what the pastor was saying, he felt his shoulders relax a little more. He realized how much he had missed this. Learning about God. Worshiping.

And with Ryann and Erica beside him, he was enjoying it even more.

Bringing his focus back to the sermon, he caught the words, "... walk humbly."

Richard watched as the pastor moved out from behind the pulpit and began pacing the stage as he continued. "Our God doesn't require much. It may seem like there is a long list of do's and don'ts once you accept Christ into your life, but there really isn't."

That wasn't what Richard remembered. He seemed to recall long lists of both growing up. Don't have fun. Don't listen to rock music. Obey your parents. And the list had seemed never ending. At least that was how it had seemed when he'd been a teenager.

The pastor paused for a moment, letting the words sink in before resuming. "The Westminster Shorter Catechism asks, 'What is the chief end of man?'"

Richard's eyebrows rose at the question. His chief end right now was to save his uncle's farm. He was on his way, but he still had a long way to go.

The pastor continued. "And the answer is this, 'Man's chief end is to glorify God, and enjoy Him forever.' Simple enough, right?"

Chuckles came from a few people in the congregation. Even Richard had to smile briefly before his thoughts turned to how he'd lived his life over the last few years. He hadn't glorified God in anything, least of all in how he'd lived his life. He hadn't even tried to follow the teaching from his youth. It had seemed impossible, so why even bother to try? He shifted again, suddenly uncomfortable. There were things he'd done to get ahead in his career where he hadn't acted honorably.

During one of the first summers he spent in Haven, he'd attended Vacation Bible School in this very church. It was during one of those times when he'd decided to follow Christ. And yet, when he'd gone home, he fell away from doing anything about it. Sure, he attended church when he was in Haven, but never anywhere else.

And now? Something seemed to call to him to change that. To change his life. To follow God fully. What would that even look like?

It was almost as if the pastor was reading Richard's mind as he continued with the sermon. "So, how are we to glorify God? What was Micah trying to convey in this message?

"We do that by living out Micah 6:8, our primary verse for today. Let me read it to you once more. 'He has told you, O man, what is good; and what does the Lord require of you but to do justice, and to love kindness, and to walk humbly with your God?'"

His thoughts in a tumble, Richard began to really examine his life. He hadn't been walking humbly or with much kindness. Until he'd come back to Haven. There was something about this place that made him want to do all that and more.

He glanced at Ryann. And someone that seemed to encourage him to be better even without saying anything. He admired Ryann's strength and her integrity. She lived a life just as the pastor had outlined.

Pastor Peter continued. "It's simple when it comes right down to it. Micah was telling the nation of Israel how they had failed to follow the Lord's steps in guiding them as a nation. He was reminding them what it would take to follow God. And we should take that same reminder to heart now.

"The Lord requires us to walk with Him. And when we do that, we become more like Christ. And when we become more like Christ, we will yearn for justice and mercy and kindness. If our heart is striving to be like Christ, then so will our actions. Our chief end is to glorify God and when we do so, we become more like him. That should be our primary goal in life. Join me in prayer."

Richard closed his eyes, but he didn't hear the words. All he could focus on was how his actions hadn't honored Christ. And he very much wanted to do that going forward. As the minister continued with his prayer, Richard said one of his own to himself. *Lord, forgive me for not following You humbly. Help me do so from this point forward. I want to know the truth of Your ways. Help me. Guide me as I try to save the farm. And if You have plans for Ryann and me, could you let me know? Thanks. Amen.*

He felt as if an enormous weight had tumbled off his shoulders as he opened his eyes and stood for the last song. He glanced at Ryann as they sang. Was he being presumptuous, asking God to help him with her?

Richard looked up at the pastor. Maybe he should get some advice on how this whole "walk humbly" thing worked. He pondered the thought as the song swelled around him.

"I'll be outside with Josie!"

Erica's exclamation brought Richard back to the present. When had the song ended? All around him, people were gathering up their belongings and heading toward the exit.

"Coming?" Ryann stood at the end of the pew looking at him with an eyebrow raised.

"In a minute. I, uh, I need to talk with someone. I'll meet you outside."

"You're being a little mysterious."

"I'll explain later. Give me ten minutes?"

"Sure." She gave him a quick grin before turning to walk up the aisle.

As Richard sat back down, he stared ahead, lost in thought about the changes he needed to make. His primary concern was how those things might impact his relationship with Ryann.

He'd realized his relationship with Sloane was never genuine. Richard had always been playing a role to conform to Sloane's expectations. But now, he craved a genuine connection with someone, where he could express himself freely and authentically, without fear of judgement or rejection.

He loved having Ryann and Erica at the farm. He didn't want it to end. The work that had seemed so overwhelming when he'd first arrived, he now found enjoyable. Each morning he woke, he looked forward to the day and spending time with Ryann. He hated the days when she worked at the café instead. It was too quiet, too lonely.

"Hi, I'm Drew. I haven't seen you here before."

Startled, Richard looked up at the guy standing in front of him with a hand outstretched. Richard grasped it, shaking it even as he stood. "I'm Richard. Richard Mosely. And it's my first time here."

"Well, nice to meet you, Richard. Welcome to Haven and to Seaside Chapel."

"Thanks." Richard opened his mouth. Maybe the guy who led worship could answer his questions for him, but then closed it again. He'd wait for the pastor.

Drew asked, "What?"

"Nothing," Richard replied.

"Are you sure? I'm happy to help if I can."

Well, it wouldn't hurt to get more than one opinion. "What does it mean, practically speaking, to walk humbly with God?"

Drew ran a hand through his hair and blew out a breath. "It means you ask Him to guide you. You don't want to go off doing your own thing without praying about it."

"Okay, but do you really pray before you do anything? Wouldn't that just take up too much time?"

"You don't have to stop to close your eyes and pray all the time. You can keep your eyes open and go about your life, but you can keep up a conversation with God. Think of it like that. Talking with God constantly."

The pastor stepped up next to Drew and stretched out his hand. "Hi, I'm Peter."

Drew clapped a hand on Peter's shoulder. "Thank goodness, help me out here, bro. I'm messing this up. This is Richard, by the way."

Richard shook the hand Peter extended to him. "Sorry, I'm just trying to figure out what you meant by walking humbly with God."

"It all starts with one simple question," Peter said. "Are you a believer of Christ and what He did when He came to earth to save us, Richard?"

"I am," Richard said with confidence. "Now what do I do?" The lightness in his spirit almost made him laugh out loud, but he refrained and just let a smile fill his face.

"Now, you seek to build your relationship with Christ. When you do that, everything else falls into place. It may not be easy, but if you trust God with everything, He'll always show you the way."

"Any chance I could take you guys out to lunch and talk about this more?"

"I've never turned down a free meal," Drew said. "Lead the way!"

"Sure, I'd love to join you," Peter said. "Let me just lock up. I can meet you at the Three Cats Café in, say, ten minutes?"

"Perfect." Richard shook both of their hands again and headed out the door. He saw Ryann waiting by the car and slowed. Erica squatted nearby, admiring a bug crawling on her finger.

He'd just invited the pastor and Drew to lunch. And he'd totally forgotten he'd driven in with Ryann this morning. What an idiot. Well, maybe she wouldn't mind joining them.

Richard smiled as he walked towards them. "I hope you don't mind. I just invited Peter and Drew to come to lunch. Is that okay?"

"Sure. Unless it's guy talk. Then Erica and I can sit at another table."

"I want to sit with Mr. Richard!" Erica exclaimed, launching herself at Richard and hugging him around the waist.

He laughed down at the little girl. "No worries, kiddo." Looking back up at Ryann, he explained, "I had some questions about the sermon, and they offered to talk with me about it. I thought the least I could do was offer to buy them lunch. And I'd love for you to join us."

"In that case, we'd enjoy that."

Richard opened the passenger door for Ryann, who slipped inside. He helped get Erica settled into the back before hurrying around to the driver's side. Smiling at Ryann as he slid into the driver's seat, he started the car. He could get used to this, having Ryann and Erica with him, eating out together. Almost like a family.

His mind continued to whirl with all the fresh revelations in his life. Today felt like a turning point, and he was eager to see what happened next.

Sixteen

Ryann

"O rder up!"

In a hurry, Ryann made her way to the counter to pick up the order for table three. The café had been busier than normal today. Between Memorial Day weekend and the Summer Festival that was in full swing, the Little League championship was scheduled for later in the afternoon. On top of everything, they were also short a waitress. It was all hands-on deck today.

She struggled to keep her mind on the job, but she kept thinking back to last Sunday when Richard had grilled Peter for over an hour on what it meant to live a life for Christ. Every question he asked led to another and another and another.

Ryann had been content listening to the men talk. It allowed her to study Richard without him being aware of it. He was too engrossed in the discussion with Peter to notice her. Richard had even asked to go to church with her again tomorrow.

She needed to focus on her job instead of wondering what the implications of Richard's newfound faith might be. Being equally yoked in marriage was crucial, and although her marriage to Eric had ended prematurely, they'd always shared the belief that Christ was fundamental.

Setting the plates in front of the couple at the table, Ryann asked, "Can I get you anything else?"

"We're all set. Thanks."

As Ryann turned to walk away, she saw the man reach for the woman's hand. The couple bowed their heads to bless the food before eating. That's what she wanted. Someone to hold her hand and pray with her. Someone to help her raise Erica. She just wanted to feel special to someone.

Taking a deep breath, she slipped down the hallway to check on Erica. Her daughter hadn't felt well this morning. There were only a few days left before summer vacation. And she still didn't have a babysitting plan in place other than bringing Erica to work with her.

Her daughter's blood sugar had been on a rollercoaster today, and Ryann wanted to keep a close eye on her. It was on days like this when she wished for extra help. She wished she had someone to come alongside her and give her a hug. Someone who would tell her it would be okay. Someone to share the burden with.

She opened the door to the office to find Erica stretched out on the couch reading. She turned her head lazily towards Ryann as she entered.

"Hi, Mommy. Are you done?"

"Not yet, sweetie. I still have a few more hours. How's the book?"

Erica shrugged. "It's okay. I'm hungry."

"Let's see where you're at first."

Her daughter rose and pulled her testing kit out of her backpack. Bringing it to Ryann, she said, "You do it."

Ryann smiled even as she thought about how this was the life ahead of her little girl. Thousands of blood samples over her lifetime to keep this disease in check.

The two bent their heads over the meter. Erica smiled up at her mom after the number on the screen popped up. 70.

"Alright then. How about a grilled cheese sandwich and some broccoli?"

"Mommy! Broccoli doesn't go with grilled cheese!" Erica turned her little nose up at the suggestion.

"Well, what does?"

"Carrots."

Ryann hid a smile. No need to argue with her daughter if she wanted to swap one veggie for another.

"Carrots it is. C'mon." She reached out her hand and helped tug her daughter towards the door. "Let's go rummage you up some vittles."

"That's what Ma says to Laura sometimes!" Erica skipped alongside Ryann as they made their way to the kitchen.

Abigail looked up as they entered. "There's my favorite kiddo! What will it be?"

"Grilled cheese, please! And some carrots!" Erica clambered up on the stool Abigail kept for her in the kitchen, folding her hands as she sat to wait.

"Coming right up!" Abigail went to get the ingredients for Erica's lunch.

"Here, drink this while you wait for your food." Ryann handed her daughter a glass of milk, and Erica took a long swallow.

Ryann said, "Let me give you your shot, kiddo." She quickly drew up the insulin her daughter would need to cover the carbohydrates in her lunch and drink. She waited for Erica to lift her shirt and push the top of her pants down so that Ryann could access her stomach.

Swiping an alcohol wipe over a spot on Erica's stomach, Ryann waved her hand to dry the area. "Ready?"

"Yup." Erica closed her eyes tight, and Ryann pushed the needle in and depressed the plunger to give her daughter the life-saving hormone. She'd started saying a brief prayer of thanks every time she did it. Thankful for the discovery of insulin. Thankful that her daughter didn't fight her about it. Thankful for so much.

Abigail slathered butter on slices of thick bread and laid them on the griddle. She placed thick slices of cheese next.

"Are we sticking with the regular grilled cheese or are we adding anything else, little one?" Abigail asked as she flipped the quickly browning bread.

"Just cheese. Don't forget my carrots!" Erica giggled as she sat watching Abigail make her lunch.

Ryann loved the sound of her daughter's giggle. "Feel free to send her back to the office to read, Abigail. She doesn't need to stay out here with you."

"Oh, I don't mind. I don't see my grandkids as often as I would like. She reminds me of one of my granddaughters. It's always good to have young energy around. It helps make the day go by faster."

"If you say so." Ryann couldn't help the sigh that escaped. "I just find it exhausting."

Abigail laughed as she finished putting together Erica's lunch. "It can be that too, absolutely." She winked at Ryann. "But that's the part they don't tell you. Being a grandparent can be exhausting, but we get to send them home, so we get a full night's sleep."

Ryann forced a laugh. She knew Abigail was just trying to help, but the smile slid off her face. She watched as Abigail placed the plate of food in front of Erica, and her little girl bowed her head to say a blessing over it.

She loved Erica, and she never regretted having her in her life. Not for a single moment. She just wished Eric hadn't died so soon after their marriage. Ryann regretted how he'd never met his daughter or how he wasn't here now to help her raise Erica.

No, if she was honest with herself, she was mad at Eric. Mad at him for leaving her here all alone. Mad at having to raise their daughter without him.

"What's wrong, Ryann? Are you okay?"

Ryann startled to find Abigail in front of her, concern etched across her face. She placed a hand on Ryann's arm, giving it a squeeze.

"Oh, just having a pity party. It's nothing," Ryann said.

"Want to talk about it?"

Sighing once more, Ryann shook her head, but the words spilled out before she could stop them. "It's hard being a single parent." Shrugging her shoulders, she gave Abigail a sad smile. "I just miss having a partner in life."

"I can understand that. We're made to be part of a couple. That's how God created it to be from the very beginning. 'A man shall leave his father and his mother and hold fast to his wife.'"

"I think I'm just destined to go this alone."

Abigail arched an eyebrow at her. "Oh really? Alone. And who is that handsome man I've been seeing you with? The one little Erica here can't stop talking about."

"Richard? He's leaving once he sells the farm. I'm just helping him get things ready, and he's helping me out of a tough spot."

"The tough spot you never told us about? The one where you were living in your car?" Abigail's eyebrow went back up.

"Um, yeah. That one." Ryann felt her face redden. "I'm sorry! I thought I had it under control."

"Living in an abandoned barn is not having it under control, sweetie. And you take away our blessings when you make those decisions for us. We're called to help each other. It's biblical, dear. So, if you're ever in a bind like that again, you'd better ask for help."

Ryann loved and hated how these women who owned the café could reduce her to feeling like a child in two seconds. And yet, she knew they did it out of love.

"We love you, sweet Ryann. We care about you." Abigail enveloped Ryann in a hug.

Ryann closed her eyes and soaked up the feeling of comfort. "Thank you," she whispered to Abigail. "Thank you for all you've done for us."

Stepping back, but keeping her hands on Ryann's arms, Abigail said, "You're welcome, sweetie. And I have one more thing to say."

"I'm not sure I want to hear it," Ryann laughed.

"You may not, but that won't stop me." Abigail joined her in laughing. "Here it is anyway... don't discount the people the Lord brings into your life. All the circumstances in your life to this point had a reason. What if it was to lead you to someone special? Someone like Richard? Think about it."

"Order up!"

The shout startled Ryann, making her jump. "I need to get back out there." She started towards where the food for her table was sitting under the warming lights, but turned back to Abigail first. "Thank you, Abigail. I promise I'll think about it."

As Ryann hurried back out front, she considered what Abigail had said. Losing her husband so soon and so young didn't seem God ordained. But then again, neither did the sin filled world they lived in. She knew God could redeem any situation and turn it around for good.

Maybe she needed to consider it all a bit more as she kept getting to know Richard again. He wasn't the same young boy she'd once known. Then again, she wasn't the same girl either. Life had changed them both. Maybe she needed to be a bit more open to a relationship with him.

And she realized she was okay with that. More than okay.

Seventeen

Richard

Richard sat at the kitchen table, head in hand. He was going to fail his uncle. He didn't know how Uncle Art thought he'd be able to turn the farm around. It was taking forever to get everything sorted out. Richard had thought this would be a quick project before arriving. It was turning into anything but.

He'd hoped to have everything done by now, but just cleaning out the house was taking longer than planned. His four-week schedule was now moving into its sixth week. The second floor was all cleaned out, even the closets, but there were still spaces on the main floor as well as the attic and basement that had yet to be touched.

Ryann had been fantastic. She worked tirelessly, even on the nights when she'd already worked a full shift on her feet at the café. He was enjoying his time getting to know her as well as Erica. The little girl was worming her way into his heart with every random question she asked.

He thought back to the other night when Ryann had come into the kitchen to make dinner. BLTC sandwiches. He smiled as he remembered how Ryann had looked up at him like he was the best thing she'd ever seen. He couldn't recall the last time a woman had looked at him that way. Maybe never. Sloane certainly never had.

Richard had realized that Sloane had always appeared slightly annoyed with him, not only in his words but also by his mere presence. It wasn't something he even realized until he saw how Ryann looked at him. It was as if she could stare into his eyes for days. And he was starting to feel the same way about her.

He'd also realized how Sloane's outlook on life was negative. Ryann laughed more. She never once complained about the hard work of hauling boxes, especially all the ones that had been stuffed in that third room upstairs. The atmosphere was more joyful when she was around. Considering how little Ryann and Erica had and the hardships they faced, their happiness was often contagious. He wanted more of it in his life.

A smile crossed his face once more at the memory. He wasn't even mad at Erica for the interruption. Except he'd been about to ask Ryann out on a date. He wanted a time with Ryann when he wouldn't need to worry about the little girl interrupting him if he wanted to kiss her mother. Not like the other night when Erica had yelled, and Ryann left before he could finish his question.

The smile faded as he looked at the papers spread on the kitchen table in front of him. He was supposed to be focusing on the farm and its finances. He needed to figure out a way for the farm to earn more income. Just harvesting the apples wasn't enough to keep it going.

He'd been dumping in his own money for the renovations needed. While he had the resources to make the farm at least livable, he still couldn't figure out a way to earn enough revenue to sustain it long term.

He'd found his uncle's old ledgers while cleaning out the library. They hadn't provided a very promising outlook of the farm and its ability to make money. In fact, his uncle had lost money the last four years running.

Richard still didn't fully understand the problem, since his uncle hadn't kept great records. He needed to come up with a solid business plan. Otherwise, he'd be better off selling everything now, as is, before dumping any more money into renovations and expansion.

And that thought didn't sit right with him. It would mean he wouldn't see Ryann anymore. And if he sold the farm, where would she go? He couldn't do that. Not yet.

No, he needed to figure out a way to make the farm more than just, well, a farm. He still thought the plan for having some type of artisan shop might work. The biggest problem was the location. They were so far off the beaten path that he wasn't sure any tourist would find them. Marketing might prove difficult. And apple season was too short to bring in enough people. He was at a loss.

"Richard! Where are you?"

Richard jumped to his feet at the urgency he heard in Ryann's voice, almost knocking his chair over. "I'm here. In here!" He hurried toward the living room. He wasn't sure what was wrong, but he wanted to fix it. Whatever it was.

"What's wrong? How can I help?" Richard grabbed Ryann's shoulders to slow her down as she came barreling down the stairs.

"Oh!" Ryann laughed. "Sorry, I didn't mean to frighten you. I have an idea for the barn!"

Richard saw sparks flying from Ryann's eyes. She looked alive and eager about something.

He gave her shoulders a squeeze before making himself release his hold and step back. It was a little too dangerous for him to touch her. He wanted to hold her and kiss her and... he forced his thoughts aside and made himself focus.

"Tell me." He hoped his voice didn't betray his feelings.

"At work today I heard something that sparked an idea. It would mean adding a few things and upgrades, but I think it's doable. I really do."

"Just tell me already!" Richard grinned. She was tripping over her words in her excitement. He liked how it made her eyes sparkle and her cheeks flush.

"What if you renovated the barn into a wedding venue?" Ryann tripped over the words as she hurried to share her idea. "I can already picture it. The room I stayed in would make a fabulous changing room for the bridal party. Add some long mirrors, a couch, and a vanity with mirrors where the workbench is. There's even room for a bathroom."

Richard considered the possibility. He knew nothing about running a wedding venue, but he thought the idea was worth exploring.

Ryann continued to outline her plan. "You could easily turn one of the other stalls into a changing room for the men with an attached bathroom. Could you connect two stalls, so one was a changing room, and one was a large bathroom? I think that might work."

Ryann began pacing in front of him as she continued to spill her thoughts. "You'd need to add some modern bathrooms for the other guests, too. While Erica loved it, I don't think any guest would want to use the outhouse unless they were going for a *really* rustic theme."

"I like the idea. But the renovations are going to be beyond my rudimentary skills."

Ryann waved a hand away. "No problem. I think Drew would take it on. The project might be too big, but if it is, he'll tell you. He knows how to fix anything." She waved her hand, as if dismissing any problem that dared to arise.

Richard stepped forward and gave into the impulse he'd been trying to keep in check since Ryann had burst in and started talking. He laid a finger against her lips. "Shhhh, I love the idea. I'll track down Drew and start working up a plan. It's brilliant. Just like you."

Ryann's eyes widened as Richard talked, keeping his finger on her lips, pressing lightly. Now, he let his hand slide over to cup her cheek and leaned forward. He just needed one small taste. One taste would be enough, he was sure.

Just as his lips brushed Ryann's, he heard a little voice exclaim, "What are you guys doing? Are you kissing?"

Richard's head whipped around. Erica stood in the door to the kitchen, hands on hips, eyes wide.

He turned back to Ryann, who was blushing from chin to hairline and biting her lower lip.

This little girl had impeccable timing. He was going to have to see what he could do about finding a moment with Ryann, alone, without a chance of interruption.

"Go out with me. Tonight. Can you find a sitter?" Richard leaned in to whisper the words to Ryann.

Her head came up and their eyes locked. He could see her thinking about it and saw the resignation come into her eyes. She was going to say no.

"Please." Richard was not above begging. This was the second time Erica had interrupted them. He didn't want to chance a third one.

Ryann glanced over to where her daughter still stood. She looked back at Richard and gave him a small smile. "I'll see what I can do. No promises. If I can find some place for Erica to go for a couple of hours, I'll go out with you Richard Mosely."

Eighteen
Ryann & Richard

Ryann couldn't believe she'd caved. It had been too easy to break the vow she'd made to herself to never date until Erica was older. But here she was, sitting beside Richard as they drove to Ellsworth. On a date. What had she been thinking?

The truth was, she hadn't. When Richard had leaned into kiss her, she'd closed her eyes and held her breath in anticipation. She'd wanted nothing more than Richard's lips on hers in that moment.

Although Ryann was still mortified at her daughter catching her. It had all happened so fast. One minute she was babbling on about her idea to turn the barn into a wedding venue and the next Richard had pulled her closer.

She glanced at the man sitting beside her. Richard had one hand on the steering wheel and one laying on the console between them. He'd shaved again before taking her out. She wished he'd left the scruff. She liked it.

There was a small bit of shaving cream near his ear. She raised her hand to wipe it away, but stopped midway.

"What is it?" Richard glanced over at her.

Ryann felt herself beginning to blush. It felt too intimate, but he was looking at her, waiting for a response.

"Oh, well, you still have a bit of shaving cream, just there." She pointed to the spot near her own ear. Richard reached up quickly to wipe it away.

"Did I get it?"

She nodded. Unable to speak. This is what she'd been missing since Eric had been gone. The everyday ordinary. The little things you did when you were in a relationship.

Wait. She wasn't starting a relationship. This was a date. Just one date. It didn't mean she was going to marry this guy.

Her head whipped over to look at Richard again before she forced her eyes back to the front. She wasn't about to let one handsome man change everything. Ryann snuck another glance and felt her cheeks flush. She had to pull herself together before Richard noticed.

"What's wrong? You look upset."

Ryann jumped. Shoot. So much for Richard not noticing. She loosened the grip she had on her skirt. She placed her hands in her lap, forcing herself to appear relaxed. "Oh, nothing. It's nothing."

"Let's do something," Richard said, keeping his gaze on the road. "Let's promise to always be honest with each other. I don't know about you, but I don't want to spend the night analyzing every word we speak to find the truth behind it." He glanced at her with a smile. "How does that sound?"

Sighing, Ryann replied, "That sounds good."

"So, why are you upset?" Richard raised one perfect eyebrow at her.

A laugh escaped before Ryann could stop it. "Fine. You want honesty? Here it is. I made a promise to myself after Eric died I wouldn't date until Erica was older."

"How old does she have to be?"

"Old enough to not care anymore." Ryann shrugged and gave a giggle. A giggle. What was wrong with her? Sobering, she continued. "I don't want Erica to become attached to someone, have the relationship fail, and have her feel abandoned. She already lost one father. I don't want her to lose anyone else."

Quiet fell between them, and Ryann turned to watch the scenery go by. The sun was low in the sky, but they still had a few hours before sunset. She knew it had been foolish to agree to the date, but Richard had caught her unaware. She hadn't had time to come up with an excuse not to come.

Part of Ryann had almost hoped Abigail wouldn't be able to watch Erica tonight. The other part hoped she could. She just prayed nothing would go wrong. Abigail understood everything she needed to do to keep Erica's blood sugars in check. Still, Ryann sent up a quick prayer. *Lord, please keep my little girl safe tonight.*

"Ryann, I promised you honesty, so here it is." Richard reached across and took her hand, squeezing it before setting their clasped hands on the console between them. "I can't promise you that our relationship will go anywhere. It might not, but I'm hoping it does."

Once more, Richard squeezed her hand as he caught her gaze before turning it back to the road. Without looking at her, he raised her hand to his mouth to press a kiss to the back of it. Ryann felt the butterflies come to life in her stomach.

Richard continued, "But I think you may be doing a disservice to Erica with your promise."

She raised an eyebrow at him, but let him keep talking. The butterflies were still going.

"What if by being in a relationship with me," he winked at her before continuing, "you're teaching Erica what it means to be with someone? What if you can teach her what it really means to love someone, including all the good and the bad?"

Love. Had Richard just said he loved her?

Richard needed to stop talking. He'd just told Ryann he loved her. Hadn't he? Did he? This was only their first date, but he already felt like he knew Ryann. They'd essentially been living together for weeks, even if it was platonic.

Weeks. Had it only been weeks? In that time, Ryann felt like the perfect fit.

Clearing his throat, Richard decided he needed to change the topic before he said anything else. And fast. "Tell me about Drew Grant. Do you think he's capable of bringing your vision for the barn to fruition?"

Richard still held onto Ryann's hand. He didn't want to let go. He risked a glance at her and saw her staring ahead, a furrow in her brow as she considered his question.

"Yeah. I mean, he's not a big contractor or anything. He's just a handyman, or that's how he puts himself out there. But I heard some guys talking this morning at the café about how Drew was working on Mr. Bush's house. From the sounds of it, he was framing an addition and, I don't know, doing stuff to make it better."

She glanced at him and gave a rueful smile. "I don't know much about building or renovating or anything. I just have this vision in my mind of what it could be. I just don't know how to make it look like what I'm picturing."

"Tell me more. You mentioned a few things, but what about food? How would we handle that? What else would we need?" Richard considered it a team effort. It was his barn, but it was her idea.

He wanted to spend the rest of the drive to the city, listening to Ryann talk. He loved her voice and her energy. Especially when she was talking about things she liked. Her passion flowed out through her entire body.

Ryann turned toward him, but she didn't release his hand. "The stalls would need to be converted. Bathrooms would need to be added."

"There are what, six stalls down each side?"

"Five, not counting the room Erica and I were staying in. Five stalls on one side, and five on the other, plus the bonus room. I think it would be easy enough to convert them." Ryann's voice filled with excitement.

"Paint me a picture. I'm listening." Richard focused on the drive as Ryann shared her vision. He hadn't felt this content in a long time.

"Starting on the right side as you enter, make that first stall an office. A place where the coordinator can meet with prospective couples and run the wedding venue."

"A coordinator, huh? Who would that be?"

"No idea. We can figure that out later." Ryann waved her hand and kept going, dismissing his question.

Richard held back a chuckle as the words continued to flow from the woman beside him.

"We could combine the next two stalls into one large lounge area. Some place where guests could sit out of the way. Maybe have a couple of couches in there with some rugs on the floor. We could make it cozy."

"Cozy. Check. Ow!" Richard jumped as Ryann punched him in the arm. "What was that for?"

"Don't be patronizing." She gave him a mock glare before smiling. "Now listen."

Richard laughed. "Fine. No patronizing. Check." He dodged towards the driver's side window to get out of reach just in case another punch came his way. "Continue."

Ryann huffed, but laughed as she continued. "I think the room Erica and I stayed in would make an excellent changing area for the bride and her party. The next stall could be converted to an attached bathroom. If you put in a few lighted mirrors, chairs, and plenty of seating, it would be fantastic.

"And the last stall on that side?"

"Yeah, install a public ladies' room. That way, the two bathrooms would be on the same side. I think that would make it easier for plumbing, right?"

Richard was getting on board with the idea. "Probably. What about the other side? What are your thoughts there?"

"Okay." Ryann's eyes shined with excitement. "This is where it all comes together.

"The first two stalls on the other side could be converted into a changing area for the guys, along with a bathroom for them. It would be near the 'front' of the venue so it would be easy enough for the groom to be where he needs to be for the ceremony without walking through all the guests."

"Does that matter? How many weddings have you been to?" Richard was curious. He hadn't really paid attention to the details of the weddings he'd attended so far.

"A lot. Anyway, the next stall would be the public men's bathroom. Again, putting the two bathrooms on that side near each other."

"That makes sense. What about the last two?"

"I'm getting there. We'll need a kitchen area. Turn the last two stalls into a prep area."

Richard's eyebrows went up. "Cooking? In an old barn? I'm not sure how safe that would be."

"Not cooking, really. I don't think we'll need a commercial kitchen since we won't provide the food, just the venue. Guests would have to have it catered. But it could have a fridge and maybe a microwave or two along with counter space to prep the food. It's just a place for the caterers to get things ready to serve."

Richard loved how Ryann had continued with the use of the word "we" throughout her explanation. It made his heartbeat just a little faster at what it would be like to work on this project with her.

"What about the middle? What are your thoughts there?" Best to keep his focus on the plan rather than what Ryann might have meant by that little word.

"That's the best part."

Richard glanced over to see Ryann almost bouncing in her seat as she laid out the last part of her plan.

"We could hang some white gauzy material to create a false ceiling. It would lower the barn ceiling just a little to make it cozier. Then hang white twinkle lights *everywhere*. And I mean everywhere. We could wrap the beams, drape them along with the material. Otherwise, I think there will be too many dark corners.

"Agreed." Richard nodded along. It was a good plan. "We'd need to install more lighting. A few well-placed lights would work. We'll have to do a lot of rewiring anyway as we renovate the stall areas."

"If we found some type of vintage chandelier or two to give more light, that would add even more character. Add in some round white tables, white chairs, more gauzy white fabric draped around. It will be beautiful."

Richard smiled. "It's a brilliant plan, but I know nothing about running a wedding venue. I've never been married. And I've only been to weddings as a guest. It might be too much."

"I don't think it will be as bad as you think. Let's talk to Drew before you decide against it."

"Do you think we can make it happen?"

Richard pulled into the restaurant and put the car in park. Turning to Ryann, he lifted her hand to his lips and pressed a kiss there. "We can certainly try."

Nineteen

Richard

"S o, tell me about Eric." Richard took a sip of his drink and waited. While he wanted to know more about Ryann's background, he wasn't sure how many details he wanted to hear. He didn't need to be jealous of her late husband. He set his glass back down, careful not to bang it.

"There's not a lot to tell." Ryann shrugged her shoulders. "He's been gone longer than he was in my life."

They'd spent most of the meal talking about various designs for the barn, finally settling on Ryann's original vision. It would now all depend on building codes and contractors. He just needed to make sure the renovations were done and the venue was turning a profit, along with the farm, by his uncle's deadline.

"Where did you meet him?" Richard asked. If Ryann's heart was still attached to her deceased husband, then this relationship was doomed before it ever started. And he really wanted to see where it might lead.

"We met at a beach party."

Richard raised an eyebrow at her. "You don't strike me as the party type."

"I'll take that as a compliment. I think." She smiled at him.

"Go on," he smiled back in encouragement.

"It was a few years after I graduated high school. I was working to save money for college. Eric was a couple of years older and from Haven, too. I knew who he was, but we never really walked in the same circles. When he showed up that night, I was just instantly taken. And for some reason, I caught his eye as well."

"I can understand that." Richard winked at her before taking a sip of his water. There was something about Ryann that made him want to dive headfirst into a new relationship. With her.

"Anyway, we hit it off and started dating. And before I knew it, we were engaged and then married. All within a year." Ryann twirled a piece of her hair around a finger as she talked.

"Seems awfully fast." Richard usually analyzed and came at the situation from every angle.

Now, ever since he'd stumbled on Ryann and her daughter in his barn that fateful night, he was moving faster than ever before.

Ryann continued with her story. "It was. But Eric was in the military. He was home on extended leave after a deployment. His unit had already been deployed overseas once and, rumor had it, they were going to be called up again. Sure enough, shortly after he proposed, he got his new orders. We eloped to the courthouse the same day."

"That must have been tough."

"It was. It was even tougher when I found out a week after he'd left that I was pregnant with Erica. A month after that, I received the notification he'd been killed in action." Ryann stopped, swallowing hard. "Sorry, sometimes it still hits me how much Erica and I lost when Eric died."

"I'm sorry. So, Eric never met his daughter?"

"No. I had one call with him during that time, and he knew I was expecting, but nothing else. He didn't even know he was going to have a daughter."

"How long were you married?"

"Just six months. But we only lived together for about three weeks."

Richard didn't know what to say. He knew people had been married for shorter periods of time. He seemed to recall a celebrity or two being married for mere hours. Ryann's marriage had been long enough to create a child. But now, she'd been a widow far longer than she'd been married.

"It must be hard to raise Erica alone."

"At first, I had help. My parents were still here, and they helped when she was a baby so I could work. But then, well, then they died too when Erica was around four years old. My dad was in a terrible car accident on the way home from work one day. Six months later, my mom died from pancreatic cancer. She went quick."

Richard reached across the table and took Ryann's hand, squeezing it. "I'm sorry. You've had a lot of loss in your life."

"Yeah," she gave a shaky laugh. "Just makes me stronger. I guess." She shrugged a shoulder. "But we do okay."

"Which is why you were living in my barn when we first met." Richard smiled and squeezed her hand.

"Well, we were still doing okay. Not great, but okay." Smiling, she slipped her hand out from under his to take another sip from her water glass. Her eyes glistening with unshed tears.

Richard already missed the touch of her hand, but he didn't want to push things. He had wonderful memories of playing in the orchard with the younger, carefree version of Ryann. But he liked this adult version of Ryann even more.

Curious, Richard continued his questions. "Why on earth were you in my barn?"

"In a word, Stan."

"Who's Stan? Do I need to go talk with Stan? Maybe beat him up?" Richard tried to give her a mean look, like he could hold his own against whoever this Stan was. He would certainly try for Ryann.

Ryann laughed, which was the reaction Richard had been hoping for.

"No, you don't have to beat up Stan. He's just a creepy middle-aged man who thinks harassing a woman with a child and no wedding ring is fun. He made up some petty lie to get me out. I was tired of dealing with him, so I left."

"But why in my barn? Why didn't you just go rent another place?"

"Spoken by a man who's never had to worry about money." Ryann ducked her head as a flush stained her cheeks.

"Not true. I was comfortable growing up and I'm comfortable now, but I'm not rich."

Ryann said nothing as she raised an eyebrow at him.

"C'mon, don't you remember the clothes I used to wear when we were kids? All the holes in them?"

"Wasn't that the fashion?" Ryann smiled at him, and Richard felt his heart speed up just a little.

"Ha. Ha. But why my barn?"

"Why? Are you kicking me out, too?"

"What? Of course not! I love having you at the farm with me." Richard stopped once he saw the smile broadening on Ryann's face. The waiter arrived to clear the table and leave the bill.

"It's nothing nefarious. I promise you that. Diabetes is expensive. I had a nest egg saved, but after Erica's diagnosis, most of it was gone. Between her initial hospitalization and all her supplies, it's eaten up my savings fast. I'm still paying off her hospital bill. I just don't have a lot of margin in my budget."

"I'm sorry. Well, you can stay at the farm as long as you'd like. I enjoy having the two of you there."

"I appreciate the offer, but I've started looking. Once the project is done, I'll have something lined up, I'm sure."

Richard reached for his wallet and placed his credit card on the bill for the waiter. He knew having Ryann and Erica on the farm felt right. It felt, well, it felt more like a home.

And since he had called for honesty earlier, he would be honest with himself. He really hoped he'd get another chance at kissing Ryann tonight. Especially after Erica had interrupted them the first time.

As soon as the waiter returned his card and he signed the slip, he stood and helped Ryann to her feet. Tucking her arm under his, he pulled her close to his side as he escorted her from the restaurant.

His mind was already whirring as he came up with ideas about how to get her out on another date and where they could go. He just wasn't sure she'd agree again. He knew how hard it was for her to leave Erica with someone.

Richard's feelings were deeper for the woman walking beside him than they'd ever been for Sloane. His relationship with Sloane had been superficial. Tonight, he'd told Ryann more about his past than he'd ever told anyone else.

"It's still early," Richard said. "Can I talk you into some dessert? Sweet Scoops is still open."

"I promised Erica I'd pick her up before bedtime. I don't want Abigail to think I'm taking advantage of her. Besides, I'm still pretty full from dinner. Maybe another time?"

Richard hoped he hid his disappointment. "Sure. How about tomorrow night? We can even bring Erica."

Richard would have to capitalize on his opportunity tonight if he was going to have a chance of kissing Ryann without an audience. He knew just the place.

"Do we have time for a quick stop before we pick her up?"

"We? I thought I'd go back out to get her after we got home."

"That doesn't make sense. Abigail's house is on the way. We can swing in and pick her up and go home together."

Gosh. Richard was falling harder and faster than he thought for this woman because just the word "home" had created a vision he would have a hard time getting out of his head. Him coming in from a long day working in the orchard. Her putting supper on the table. Erica running to throw herself into his arms as she yelled, "Yeah! Daddy's home."

Pushing the thoughts away, Richard tried again. "It won't take long. Do you trust me?"

"Of course. Lead on then, good sir!" Ryann laughed.

The sound penetrated deep into Richard's heart. He could spend a lifetime making Ryann laugh.

They fell silent as he drove back towards Haven. He spent the time planning the next few steps in his head. Richard wanted it to be perfect. He wanted to show Ryann how much she meant to him.

Slowing, he pulled onto a grass track that slowly climbed to the top of a hill. Parking, he jumped out and ran around to hold Ryann's door for her.

"Where are we?"

"Patience."

Richard held out his hand to Ryann. She hesitated only a moment before taking it and stepping out after him.

It didn't seem like she remembered the place, but he'd never forgotten. It was the spot where, almost fifteen years ago, he'd tried kissing her. They'd both been awkward teenagers. Well, he'd certainly been awkward. He didn't think Ryann had ever been.

Keeping a firm hold of her hand, he walked up the path to the top of the hill. The full moon out tonight gave them plenty of light to see where they were going. The short walk was worth it. At the top, the town of Haven lay before them. Lights blinked back at them from the houses. He looked up at the stars filling the sky. The pulsing light from Haven Light swept across the view as it rotated.

Richard pulled Ryann around to stand in front of him and wrapped his arms around her shoulders, pulling her gently back against him. "What do you think?"

"I love this spot. I always have. But I got so busy with life, I'd forgotten it until just now."

"Do you remember anything else about this spot?" Richard wasn't sure why he'd asked the question. Ryann probably hadn't given him a second thought in years. She'd married and had a child while he'd gone off and started a life. A life he was realizing he didn't want.

Turning in his arms, Ryann looked up at him. She reached a hand up and let her fingers lay at the back of his neck, tangling in his hair. Richard swallowed hard as he gazed into her eyes. In the darkness, the moon provided just enough light for him to see her looking back, a slight smile on her lips. The lips he wanted to kiss.

He swallowed hard once more, shuffling his feet. He was being transported back to that time of being an awkward teenager. Maybe this had been a bad idea.

"I remember you tried to kiss me here when we were teenagers, Richard Mosely. But we were both too scared to make it happen. Do you want to fix that?" Ryann tightened her fingers in his hair and pulled him towards her.

"More than anything," Richard murmured just before their lips met.

Try to interrupt this, Erica, he thought. Richard drew Ryann closer, his lips angling to meet hers. He knew he should hold back. He didn't want to scare her away, but he wasn't sure he could stop himself from deepening the kiss.

The sound of a phone ringing broke the night silence.

Ryann drew back.

Richard murmured, "Ignore it," as he began pulling her lips closer. He needed more.

"I can't. It might be Erica."

Sighing, Richard let her step away. Erica had interrupted them after all. He already felt the loss of Ryann from his arms.

Twenty

Ryann

♥

G runting, Ryann started dragging the old recliner from the living room toward the front door. "C'mon, Erica. Help me. Give it a push."

Erica came running and shoved the recliner hard. Ryann tried to stay focused on getting the last of the things out of the main floor, but her thoughts kept drifting back to the kiss with Richard. The one she'd even started.

The first man to show her interest had made her forget her vow. Pathetic.

Well, that wasn't entirely true. There had been other men over the years, but they'd been easy to rebuff. None of them had captured her interest like Richard. She felt safe with him. She was eager to see him again. Maybe even get another kiss.

She held back the sigh, trying to escape. All it took was one toe curling kiss, and she tossed her vow out the window. She needed to remember that her daughter came first. Always.

Ryann wrestled the oversized armchair through the doorway. She needed to get it across the yard to the dumpster. Erica was trying to help, but there was only so much a seven-year-old could do without becoming more of a hindrance than a help.

"Thanks, sweetie. We'll leave it here. Richard can help me get it in the dumpster later. You've been a good helper today. If you want to go read for a bit, I can do the rest."

"Thanks, Mommy!" Erica wrapped her arms around Ryann's waist and squeezed before running off. Ryann could hear her feet pounding up the stairs as she headed to her room to get her newest book.

The dumpster was already half-filled with broken furniture, old boxes of tax returns, and other miscellaneous papers. She'd even tossed out a shoebox filled with receipts for prescriptions filled over ten years ago.

All these weeks later, she was still finding stuff in odd places. Random things like empty pill bottles with the labels removed or piles of used soap stuffed in old mason jars.

The first floor was almost empty enough to start the next step of the renovations. Tonight, she and Erica would start removing the wallpaper from the dining room walls. The wallpaper was circa 1970s–avocado green and harvest gold. She couldn't wait to remove it and start painting.

Her stomach flipped at just the thought of seeing Richard when he got home. He'd gone to get supplies for them over in Ellsworth. Ryann had given him a long list of things to pick up.

Pushing thoughts away about how she could get another kiss from Richard tonight once Erica was in bed, Ryann turned back to the task at hand. She needed to finish emptying the room so they could start ripping down the wallpaper.

"Where did you go with Richard last night? Can I come next time?" Erica stood in the doorway to the living room, waiting for Ryann to answer.

"I thought you were upstairs reading."

"I didn't have that much left. I finished it and wanted a snack. So, where did you go?"

"I told you we went to dinner in Ellsworth. And yes, you're coming with us the next time we go. I told you that, too." Ryann ran a hand down her daughter's hair. "Why all the questions?"

"I just don't want you to forget to take me next time." Erica shrugged and smiled at her mom.

Ryann shook her head. "I promise I won't forget you. Do you want to help me move the couch?"

"Sure. Then can I have a snack?"

"Yes, then you can have a snack."

Ryann stood, hands on hips, eying the couch that remained. She hefted one end, trying to judge if she'd be able to get it outside on her own. She pulled the cushions up and discovered it was a convertible sofa.

Holding back a groan, she thought for a minute. Then Ryann said, "Erica, run and grab me the small rugs by the back door."

Her daughter took off running and was soon back with the two area rugs.

"Okay, I'm going to lift this end of the couch." Erica pointed to one end. "When I do, I want you to put one rug under the legs of the couch."

The little girl nodded and knelt beside the couch.

Ryann leaned down and squatted, getting her hands under the edge. "I'm going to count to three. On three, scoot in there and get that rug placed nice and flat as quick as you can. Ready?"

"Ready!"

"Okay, one... two... three!" With a grunt, Ryann lifted the couch. Erica scooted closer and slid a rug under the legs.

"Hurry, honey. This couch is heavy!"

"Almost done!" With one last pat, Erica scooted back, and Ryann let the couch down with a thud.

"Okay, the other side."

Stepping back, she wiped her brow with the back of her hand. She wasn't sure her idea of pushing the couch outside was going to work, but she was still going to try. She wanted to be sure she was doing all she could to hold up her end of the bargain.

Caught by a sudden movement outside, Ryann turned to the window. As she approached, she saw an unfamiliar car pulling into the driveway. She stood still, watching to see who would step out. She wasn't in the mood for visitors, especially not covered in dirt with her hair a mess. Ryann hoped it was just a lost tourist who needed directions.

A woman wearing a tailored pair of pants and a flowing blouse stepped out and closed the door to a fancy car. Ryann didn't know what it was, but there were three little circles on the front grill. It was definitely not something she could afford.

"Hang on a second, honey. Someone's here. I'm going to see what they want. I'll be back in a minute."

"Okay, I'm going to get my snack." Without waiting for a response, Erica scurried through the door to the kitchen. Ryann heard cupboards banging as she headed out the open front door.

Stopping at the top of the porch steps, she called out, "Can I help you?"

Pushing a pair of sunglasses to the top of her head, the woman stepped to the front of the car. "Who are you? Where's Richard?"

"He's not here. Can I help you?" Ryann asked again, not like the other woman's sharp tone. She'd dealt with worse at the café, especially during the tourist season.

"You didn't answer me. Who are you?"

Ignoring the question, Ryann chose to tell this woman Richard wasn't here. Maybe then she would leave. "Richard went to get supplies. He'll be back in about an hour. I can tell him you stopped by if you tell me your name."

Ryann fought the urge to snatch the bandana off her head and wipe her face. She was sure she had streaks of dirt on it. Compared to the woman in front of her, she must look like a vagabond. Oh wait, she was a vagabond. One who was living here only because of the good graces of a good man.

"I'm Sloane. His girlfriend. Don't make me ask again. Who are you?" The other woman wrinkled her nose as she turned to look around the farm. "I can't believe he's living here now."

Ryann's stomach dropped. Richard had a girlfriend? And he'd said nothing. He'd acted as if he was single. And she'd kissed him. This is why she needed to hold to her vow. She wouldn't break Erica's heart over and over by men leaving. Or by men lying.

Without thinking, Ryann answered the question. "I'm Ryann. I live here, too."

The woman turned slowly to look at her. "You live here?" Her voice rose, incredulous.

"I do. With my daughter."

Ryann opened her mouth to further explain the situation, but before she could, Sloane snapped, "We'll see about that!"

The woman was in her car before Ryann could utter a word. She took a left out of the driveway. Ryann wondered how long it would take the woman to realize she was going in the opposite direction from town.

"Who was that Mommy?"

"Someone looking for Richard."

"There he is! I found him first!"

Erica jumped off the step so she could run to meet Richard. He was turning into the driveway in a rented truck. Boards sticking out of the back.

"Hold up! Let him park before you go running toward him, sweetie. It's not safe to run toward a moving vehicle. Remember?"

The little girl bounced on her toes, waving her arms over her head. Ryann wanted to smile, but she knew she would have to tell Richard they were leaving. She couldn't stay here. She didn't want Erica to get any more attached to Richard than she already was. It was time to move on, even though she hadn't finished her part of the bargain.

"You've been busy." Richard nodded at the dumpster.

"Hey kiddo!" He ruffled Erica's hair. The little girl grabbed his hand and skipped alongside him as he walked towards where Ryann was standing on the porch.

Ryann's heart picked up speed as she saw him smile. Better to start with the important things first. "Your girlfriend was here looking for you. You just missed her, but she went that way." Ryann pointed in the opposite direction from where Richard had come. "If you leave now, you can probably catch up with her." Crossing her arms, she waited.

He stopped in mid-stride as confusion crossed his face. "What are you talking about? I don't have a girlfriend."

"She said her name was Sloane. She was driving some fancy car and wearing fancy clothes looking for you on an apple farm in the middle of nowhere Maine." Ryann raised an eyebrow at him.

Richard narrowed his eyes as he looked towards the road. "Did she say what she wanted?"

"She didn't, but she seemed upset to find me here."

"I bet she did." He ran his free hand through his hair.

"I'll be out of here tomorrow. I'm sure someone at the café can find me a place in a heartbeat." Ryann turned to go back inside.

"We're leaving, Mommy? But I don't want to leave!" Erica stomped a foot. "I want to stay here with Mr. Richard!"

"Erica, that's enough," Ryann gritted through her teeth. "Go inside."

The little girl obeyed even though she slammed the door behind her.

Ryann took a deep breath. She needed to get her own anger under control before she dealt with her daughter. She turned to go inside even as she heard Richard hurrying up the steps behind her.

"Wait! Sloane isn't my girlfriend." Richard stepped forward, turning her to face him. "Don't go. I want *you* to stay."

"She doesn't seem to know that. Did you tell her?" Ryann arched an eyebrow at him.

"She broke up with me before I came to Haven. She hasn't contacted me since I left Portland. Besides, I'm not dating Sloane. I'm dating you. At least I thought I was."

Ryann closed her eyes as she let Richard draw her closer. She sighed as his arms wrapped around her and held her tight. Could she trust him? This felt so good, and she wanted him in her life.

She just prayed she wasn't setting herself up for heartbreak. Or Erica either. The last thing she wanted was her daughter's heart broken. Or her own.

Twenty-One

Richard

♥

The next afternoon, Richard sat tucked into a corner booth at the Three Cats Café, sipping a cup of coffee and people watching. He was meeting with Drew today to complete the plans for the barn. He was excited about the possibility of creating an event center.

The bonus to meeting at the café was Richard could also watch Ryann. He'd never been at the café when she'd been working before. She bustled about serving customers, never looking hurried or put out with any request. He could pick out her melodious laughter over the hum of conversation and clatter of dishes.

He took a bite of the hand pie Ryann had just dropped off, along with his coffee. Eyes closing in bliss, he chewed the bite of apple pie and swallowed.

"Am I interrupting?"

Richard's eyes flew open at the familiar low and throaty voice and found Sloane giving him a coy look. She hadn't returned to the farm, but he hadn't gone looking for her either. He'd hoped she'd left town after finding Ryann on his porch. Apparently not.

"What are you doing here? I thought you said you'd never step foot in this town."

"I missed you." She smiled at him and skimmed a finger down his arm as she slid onto the bench seat across from him. Smiling, she reached for his hand.

Crossing his arms, Richard sat back, out of reach. He wasn't interested in playing this game. Sloane had made it clear they were done.

During his time in Haven, he'd realized he was no longer interested in the same life Sloane had her eyes set on. He wanted something simpler. And something with someone who wasn't only interested in what she could gain by being with him.

He glanced to the last place he'd seen Ryann standing, but she wasn't there. He brought his attention back to Sloane. "Again, what are you doing here?"

"I told you already. I missed you. Didn't you miss me?"

She gave him a smile that made him tighten his jaw. It was the same smile that had once done the opposite. "I doubt it. If that were true, I would have heard from you before now. What gives?"

Sloane's lower lip protruded forward in what she probably thought was an adorable pout. It only made her look like a spoiled child.

"Why do I need more of a reason? We meant something to each other at one point. Maybe I want to have that again." She fluttered her eyelashes at him.

Shaking his head, Richard held back a snort. Maybe once he would have been vain and superficial enough to fall for her ploy, but not anymore. Being in Haven had taught him what genuine relationships looked like. And his relationship with Sloane hadn't been real. It had been as fake as the nails on her hands.

"Look, I don't know what your real motive is here, but your life is in Portland. You made that clear. Go home. I don't have time for games. Besides, I'm meeting someone."

"Are you meeting *her*?"

"Her who?" Richard's brow furrowed.

"That woman you're living with. I didn't catch her name, but she kicked me off the property when I went looking for you. And a child? Really, Richard. I'm surprised you went for a ready-made family like that."

Richard's lips thinned. He'd always known Sloane could be catty and petty. He'd seen her do it to others.

"Sloane, it's none of your business what I'm doing. We're not a couple anymore. Besides, I've decided I'm staying. I'm not selling the farm. In fact, I'm working to make it into something more."

Sloane burst out laughing. The noise grated on Richard's nerves.

"More than a farm? Seriously, Richard. Stop being so dramatic and come back to where you belong. I know I can convince my father to give you your job back. You won't get the promotion now, but you will eventually. We'll have to live in Portland for an extra year, maybe two, but we'll end up in New York soon enough."

Richard leaned forward, slapping his hand on the table. Sloane's eyes widened, but she closed her mouth.

"Listen to me, Sloane. I'm *not* going back to Portland with you. I'm staying in Haven. We," he pointed at his chest and then at her, "are not an item anymore. We're not dating. We're over. You walked away, remember?"

Sloane's face flushed red, and her lips thinned as she clenched her jaw. Richard had seen that look just before she lashed out at someone. Maybe she finally realized she didn't have a hold on him any longer.

"Can I get you anything?"

Richard spun his head to look up. Ryann was standing by his shoulder, pad of paper in hand, pen at the ready. Her sweet smile calmed his rising anger immediately.

"Nothing for me, and she," he nodded towards Sloane, "was just leaving." He raised an eyebrow at Sloane.

Sloane's eyes narrowed, and she leaned forward. "You'll regret not picking me someday when you realize all you gave up. See that you don't. You'll hate living in the middle of nowhere," she hissed at him. Standing, she straightened her blouse and took a step forward, getting in Ryann's face.

Richard tensed, preparing to jump between them. He wouldn't put it past Sloane to lash out at Ryann.

"You can have him. He's not worth it." Spinning, Sloane marched out of the café, pushing past customers to get to the door.

Drew slid into the seat across from Richard. "Heya, Ryann! Can I get a coffee and whatever magic Brenda has whipped up? Thanks."

Richard saw Ryann give a small jump at Drew's words before she said, "Sure thing. I'll be right back."

As Ryann made her way to the kitchen, Richard's eyes followed her every step. He felt an urgent need to chase after her and clear the air. He realized how crucial it was to him for her to understand there was nothing between him and Sloane. The truth was, he no longer wanted what Sloane had to offer. His heart belonged solely to Ryann.

"So, ex-girlfriend?" Drew smiled at Richard as he nodded at the car now screeching out of the parking lot.

"How'd you guess?"

Drew laughed. "A woman scorned is easy to spot. Tell me more about this project."

Richard chuckled. "She did the scorning, not me."

Pushing thoughts of Sloane away, he placed the notebook full of the sketches and ideas he'd put together, with Ryann's help, on the table. The two men bent their heads and started going over the practicalities of turning the barn on the apple farm into something more.

Twenty-Two

From the kitchen, Ryann peeked out from behind the door where Richard and Drew were pouring over the plans for the barn. She itched to be over there, sitting beside Richard and giving her input. But he hadn't asked.

"Who was that?"

Ryann jumped as Brenda spoke from behind her.

"Who was who?

"The blonde from the city giving Richard a hard time a few minutes ago."

"His ex-girlfriend. She stopped by the farm yesterday when he wasn't home."

Brenda gave a quiet whistle through her teeth as she plated up a frosted blueberry hand pie and handed it to Ryann. "That must have been interesting."

"You could say that. She thinks there's more between Richard and I than there really is."

Brenda gave her a small smile and nudged her toward the front. "Sometimes a city girl gets it right."

"What?"

"Go give that to Drew while it's still hot. Thanks, honey." Brenda spun on her heel and hurried toward the offices before Ryann could say anything else.

She knew her mouth was hanging open. What was Brenda implying?

Sure, she'd kissed Richard. And if she were being honest with herself, she'd enjoyed it. And sure, she was hoping for another one... or two. But they'd only gone on one date so far. While there was attraction there, she was still hesitant about the next step.

Sighing, Ryann realized maybe it was time to trust God with this situation. After all, the good Lord had to be orchestrating it. Otherwise, it didn't make sense.

She poured a cup of coffee for Drew. Taking a deep breath, she plastered a smile on her face. Was she brave enough to move forward with Richard? Or was she going to let her vow keep her single for another ten years or more?

Before she could come up with an answer, she was by the booth, sliding the plate onto the table. "Here you go, Drew. Can I get you anything else?"

"Hey, can you join us for a minute?" Richard asked as he glanced up. "Drew has some ideas and I want you to hear them and help me figure it out."

Ryann's heart soared before she tamped it back down. "Sure, let me just let Brenda know I'm taking a break. I'll be right back." She held back the giggle that tried to escape. She was acting like a lovestruck teenager.

She stumbled on her way back to the kitchen to let Brenda know she'd be off the floor for a few minutes. Lovestruck? She couldn't be in love with Richard. Not yet. They hadn't known each other long enough. Except they had their history, and that just made it seem like she'd known him forever.

"Nothing between you, huh? Yeah, right." Brenda smirked, but quickly gave a smile and a wink before she went back to rolling out pie dough.

Richard slid over as she approached, and she sat down beside him, thighs touching as he moved over to make room. She held her breath before letting it out slowly. She needed to focus and keep the giggles that kept trying to bubble up from slipping out.

The thought of being in love with Richard made her want to sing and dance and laugh. Crazy. That's what she'd look like if she acted on her feelings right now.

She needed to concentrate on what Drew was telling her. But all she could feel was the warmth emanating off Richard into her side. She wanted to snuggle closer. She felt a flush creeping up her cheeks.

Shaking her head slightly, she refocused on the plans. She needed to pay attention if she was going to share her ideas.

"You don't agree?" Drew asked, finger hovering over the lounge area.

"I'm sorry. I lost track for a minute. Can you go over that again?"

Drew began once more. "I think it makes sense to flip things around. Put the office in the back corner where you planned for the kitchen to go. I haven't seen the room yet, but from how Richard describes it, the room here," he pointed to where

Ryann had once stayed, "seems to be perfect for the women's dressing area."

Ryann felt her brow furrow as she thought of how the new design would work. "It could be. But wouldn't that put the kitchen near the front? I'm not sure it should be where the guests would enter."

"Would it matter?" Drew asked.

"Okay, so the bride needs to 'walk an aisle', right?" Richard pointed to the front barn doors as he interjected.

"Right." Drew and Ryann said together as they waited for Richard to continue.

"So, we need to figure out where that would logically be. If the wedding is outside, where would the bride come from? And if it's inside, where would she start and end? Once we figure that out, we'll know the best place for everything else. At least that's what I'm thinking."

Drew laughed. "Here we are, three single people, trying to figure out how to set up a wedding venue."

"Well, you've been married before." Richard said to Ryann. "What do you think works best?"

Ryann swallowed her laughter. "We just went to the court-house. We didn't do a large ceremony. I'm no help."

Richard placed a hand over Ryann's and squeezed. "Sorry. I didn't mean to bring up any sad memories."

She gave him a small smile. "It's okay. Marrying Eric isn't a sad memory."

Her heart gave an extra beat when Richard left his hand on top of hers. It grounded her in a way she hadn't felt since Eric had been alive. On impulse, she turned her hand over and wove her fingers through Richard's. She saw his eyes widen slightly, but he squeezed and left their clasped hands on the table.

Turning to Drew, Ryann suggested, "Why don't Richard and I look things over tonight, figure out where the outside and inside options make sense, and we'll get back to you."

"Sounds great. Now, I'm going to dive into this hand pie before it gets cold."

Ryann slid out of the bench, giving Richard's hand one last squeeze before letting go. She felt a sense of loss when she was no longer touching him. "I need to get back to work. See you at home later."

As her face warmed, Ryann hurried away. She hadn't meant to make it sound so intimate, like they lived together. But that's exactly what they did even if it was only a platonic relationship. Her face continued to heat as she hurried to the kitchen.

She glanced over her shoulder before ducking inside and caught Richard's gaze. Locking eyes with him, she once more felt grounded. She shot him a quick smile before heading back to work.

Home. She liked the sound of that.

Twenty-Three

Richard & Ryann

♥

R ichard swallowed hard as he stood in the middle of the barn watching Ryann walk slowly toward him.

"So, if the bride came from this end, this is what it would look like. What do you think?" Ryann called out.

It was easy to imagine Ryann wearing a long white dress with a veil covering her face as she strode towards him. A picture formed in his head of what he would do as the minister said, "You may now kiss the bride." He would lean in close, wrap his arms around her and...

"Richard, what do you think? Does this work for a wedding?"

He opened his mouth to reply, but before he could, a little voice shrieked, "You're getting married, Mommy? Yeah! I get a daddy!"

Erica barreled toward him from the back of the building. She'd been out playing in the orchard while Richard and Ryann worked on figuring out a solution for the barn design.

Richard blinked as the image he'd been enjoying evaporated as Erica crashed into his legs.

"You're going to be my daddy, Mr. Richard! Can I call you Daddy?"

Richard stared at the little girl, shocked. His mouth opened and closed. He must look like a fish gasping for water. He felt like it. Pulling his eyes away from Erica's pleading gaze, he tried to gauge Ryann's reaction.

She stopped where she was, a look of shock on her face, before hurrying towards them.

Tearing his eyes from Ryann's, Richard looked down once more at the little girl. It was easy to picture himself marrying Ryann, and it was all too easy to picture having Erica as a daughter.

He'd never thought of having children. At least not yet. His focus had been on his career. And Sloane had never even hinted at wanting a family. But now that he was around Erica more? He could see the draw of having a child.

Ryann's voice broke through as she stopped, pulling her daughter toward her. "No, sweetie. I'm not getting married. Mr. Richard and I were just working on the layout for the barn, so I needed to pretend to be a bride. That's all it was, just pretending."

"Oh," the little girl sighed and kicked a foot against the floorboards of the barn. "But why not? Don't you like Mr. Richard?"

Kneeling beside her daughter, Ryann glanced up and met his gaze. Richard couldn't look away. There was something in her eyes. Something he hadn't seen before. Desire? Maybe. He took a step towards her.

Ryann broke eye contact, and Richard halted. She pulled Erica in for a quick hug. Richard turned to leave but stopped. He couldn't go. He wanted to know what Ryann would say to Erica.

"I do like Mr. Richard, Erica. Very much."

Richard felt as if his heart would stop at those words. Maybe some people would say this relationship had happened too fast, but he felt he knew more about Ryann than he'd ever known about any woman, including Sloane.

"Then why? I want a daddy. Everyone I know has one. Rachel at school even has *two*—a daddy and a step-daddy. I don't have any. It's not fair!" Tears now glistened in Erica's eyes. Richard wanted nothing more than to sweep her up in a big hug and tell her it would be okay. He'd be her daddy.

Ryann glanced at him again, but turned her focus quickly back to Erica. "It doesn't work that way, honey. People can't just get married. They need to love each other first. Once they do that, then they get married."

Richard heard the break in Ryann's voice when she said the word love. Had he been wrong? Was she more hung up on her deceased husband than he'd thought?

"But you know Mr. Richard. We live in his house already. Most mommies and daddies live in the same house. I don't understand why Mr. Richard can't be my daddy."

Ryann smiled at her daughter as she smoothed the hair off Erica's face. "You're right. Most mommies and daddies live in the same house. But you can't just declare you're getting married. There's more to a relationship than that. You've got to be sure you can live with each other forever. Forever is a long time, isn't it?"

"Yeah. I guess so. But I could live with Mr. Richard forever. And I could live on this farm forever. I love it here! I don't want to leave!"

"I know it's hard, sweetie. Trust me, okay? When the time is right, God will bring a daddy into your life. And he'll be the perfect daddy for you and the perfect husband for me."

Ryann met Richard's eyes over Erica's shoulder, and he let out the breath he'd been holding.

Did Ryann really believe God would bring her a husband? Did it work like that? He'd been making his own way in the world for years. What would it be like to trust God in something as important as finding the perfect wife?

Shoulders slumping, Erica said, "Okay. I understand. God's timing is perfect. No matter what."

Ryann pulled her daughter close, laying her cheek on top of Erica's head. "It sure is, kiddo. It sure is."

"I think I need a snack."

Erica sank to the ground at Ryann's feet.

Richard stepped forward, no longer content to wait out of arm's reach. "What's wrong?"

"She's going low." Ryann scooped her daughter up and started moving to the house.

"Mommy? I don't feel so good." Erica's eyes rolled up and the little girl's head lolled to the side.

"Give her to me!" Richard didn't wait for permission. He pulled Erica into his arms and sprinted for the house with Ryann close on his heels.

He took the porch steps in two giant leaps. He managed to open the door and was through before Ryann made it up the steps to help.

"Where do you want me to put her?"

Ryann, panting at the run, directed him. "Lay her on the couch. I'll be right back."

Richard lay the unconscious child on the couch. He'd never felt so helpless in his life. "Should I call 911?" he yelled out to Ryann.

"Not yet!" Ryann came sprinting back into the room.

She skidded to a stop by the sofa and sank to the floor beside Erica. Fumbling with the testing kit, she loaded a test strip with a shaking hand. Richard wanted to help, but he knew he would just get in the way. Ryann loaded the test strip with blood. They waited for the number to pop up. 35.

"How bad is it?" Richard asked. He didn't know what the number meant.

"Call 911," Ryann yelled as she once more ran from the room.

Richard wasted no time. He yanked his phone out of his pocket, swiped it open, and dialed the three digits. He gave the dispatcher the address and details.

Ryann was back just as Richard finished speaking. She had a small red case in her hand. "Tell them I'm giving her glucagon."

He repeated the words to the dispatcher as Ryann opened the case.

With trembling hands, she removed a small syringe and vial. "Do you need help?" he asked her.

Shaking her head, no, she injected the liquid from the syringe into the vial. She removed the syringe and shook the vial to mix the tablet inside with the liquid she'd just added. Next, she drew the liquid back into the syringe. Taking a deep breath, she jabbed the needle into Erica's thigh. The little girl didn't even flinch.

Jerking his head, Richard had been so focused on what Ryann had been doing, he hadn't realized the dispatcher was yelling in his ear. "Roll her on her side!" he barked at Ryann.

Ryann pulled Erica to the edge of the couch just as the little girl's eyes fluttered open and she threw up.

Richard heard the sirens blaring as the ambulance pulled into the driveway. Thanking the dispatcher, he hurried out the door to lead the way inside.

Thanks, Dr. Adams. Yes, I will."

Ryann tapped the button on her phone to end the call. Taking a deep breath, she blinked rapidly. She wouldn't fall apart now. She refused to think of the 'what ifs.' Her daughter was safe and home again. A few hours in the emergency department had stabilized her blood sugar.

But all Ryann could think about was how she could have lost Erica. Just like that.

Laying her shaking hands on the kitchen counter, she bent forward, breathing deeply. She wouldn't cry. Not now that it was all over. Dwelling on what could have happened wouldn't change anything now. And Erica was fine.

She glanced over to where her daughter sat on the floor in the living room, playing with her dolls. Erica was the brightest point in her life. And after yesterday, she understood even more just how fast things could change.

Thank goodness Richard had been here. Ryann didn't think she would have been so calm if she'd been alone. He'd helped keep her steady, just with his presence.

"Are you okay, Mommy?" Erica slipped a hand into Ryann's and leaned into her side.

Ryann had been so engrossed in her thoughts she hadn't heard her daughter approach. "I am, honey. What about you? How are you feeling?" Ryann squatted down and pulled her daughter into her arms to give her a tight squeeze.

Erica wiggled out and smiled at her mother. "I'm good. Just a little tired."

"Too tired to help me make cookies?" Ryann needed something to focus her energy on and to take her mind off things.

"Not that tired!" Erica clapped her hands and scurried into the kitchen. Ryann followed, smiling and thanking God for keeping her daughter safe.

"Let's put on some music. What do you want to listen to?" Ryann picked her phone up and tapped to open her music app. She looked expectantly at Erica, waiting for her request.

"How about MercyMe?"

"Sure." Erica had been obsessed with the band ever since finding out the lead singer's son was also a Type 1 diabetic.

Ryann connected her phone to the Bluetooth speaker on the counter beside her and cranked up the volume. Soon the music filled the kitchen as she began pulling out the ingredients to make chocolate chip cookies.

Erica was eager to help and, while Ryann knew it would be faster and easier to do it herself, she wanted her daughter close to her today.

Ryann's heart swelled with emotions as she watched her daughter dance around the kitchen. Losing Eric had been hard enough. She couldn't bear the thought of losing their daughter as well. She was the last connection Ryann had with him.

"Hey, slow down there, kiddo. Let's get some juice into you."

Dr. Adams had warned Ryann to keep a close eye on Erica today. There might be some lingering effects from the severe low sugar from yesterday. Ryann wasn't about to take any chances.

Pulling open the fridge, she pulled out the last juice box. Flipping it end over end, she caught it and presented it to Erica with a flourish. The little girl giggled and clapped her hands.

"You're so silly, Mommy!"

"Silly, am I?" Ryann raised an eyebrow at her. "Well, maybe the silly monster needs to come out and you can see which one of us is sillier!"

Shrieking, Erica fled the room. Ryann went running after her, stomping her feet and flailing her arms around, fingers splayed like claws.

Erica was on the couch, laughing so hard she could barely sit up. "The silly monster is sillier than you, Mommy!"

Ryann flopped down beside her daughter and handed her the juice box. "Drink. Then let's get back to those cookies."

Erica took the box, finishing it quickly. She bounced back to her feet and hurried into the kitchen.

Ryann sat for a moment, catching her breath, and said a brief prayer of thanks for her daughter's life.

"Seems like I'm missing all the fun."

Ryann startled as she whirled towards the door. "Richard! I didn't hear you come in." She wondered how long he'd been standing there. "Sorry about the noise. I'll go turn down the music."

Before she could rise, Richard was there, holding out a hand to her. She eyed it and him before accepting his offer.

With a quick yank, he pulled her to her feet and right into his embrace.

"Richard!"

"The music is fine. The noise is fine. You're perfect. Erica is adorable. Do I need to cover anything else?"

Ryann stilled. "I'm not perfect, Richard. No one is. Don't put me on a pedestal."

"In my eyes, you are perfect. Nothing you say will change that."

She huffed out a laugh. "Give me time. Now let me go. I need to go check on Erica."

Richard looked over her head towards the kitchen. "She's eating chocolate bits and dancing around the kitchen. She looks fine to me."

He dropped his head and locked eyes with her.

Ryann swallowed hard, but couldn't look away. His dark brown eyes held her captivated. And in that moment, she remembered the conversation she'd had with Erica right before her daughter had collapsed. Erica wanted Richard to be her daddy. Erica wanted them to be married.

Her eyes dropped to his lips. Biting her lower lip, she forced herself to look back into his eyes. She wouldn't ask to be kissed. Her eyes dropped once more to his mouth.

"Richard, I..."

"I'm going to kiss you."

Before Ryann could say anything, Richard lowered his head and claimed her lips.

She shouldn't be kissing him where Erica would see. She... her thoughts trailed off as Richard wove his fingers into her hair. He pulled her closer, deepening the kiss. She heard a small groan, but didn't know if it came from her or from him. And right now, she didn't care.

"Mommy?"

Ryann pulled back, breaking the kiss, eyes opened in shock as she met Richard's.

"Mommy, why are you kissing Richard if you aren't married?"

Heat flooded Ryann's face. Her daughter had just caught her making out with Richard. What kind of example was she setting? What kind of mother did that?

"She has a point."

"What?" Richard wasn't suggesting what she thought he was. Was he?

"I want Richard to be my daddy. If you're kissing, doesn't that mean you should be married?"

Ryann's eyes flew to Erica and back to Richard. Stepping back quickly, she smoothed her hands down her shirt and wiped a hand over her lips. She opened her mouth to say something, but shut it. Opened. Closed.

Not knowing how to respond, she took the coward's way out. Ryann whirled and hurried up the stairs, leaving both her daughter and Richard standing in the living room.

How had she lost control like that? Ryann flopped onto her bed like a teenage girl, one arm thrown over her eyes as she replayed what had just happened. Her heart rate once more increased at the memory of what Richard's lips had felt like on hers. One hand drifted to cover her mouth, trying to trap the feeling there. And his hands in her hair, how he pulled her closer. How she'd felt safe. How every thought had fled. Even thoughts of Erica.

Her sigh filled the room. She'd crossed a line she'd set, and now she needed to figure out how to fix it. All Ryann knew was she couldn't continue living here, especially if she was going to pursue a romantic relationship with Richard. And right now, that's very much what she wanted to do.

But she needed to set an example for her daughter to follow. And living with someone before marriage was not it.

Sitting up, she began putting together a plan. She would talk with Abigail tomorrow. Either Abigail or one of her sisters would likely know of someone who had a place Ryann could rent.

But what about her agreement with Richard? She wasn't sure how much more work they had left to do. And if she was being honest with herself, she didn't want to leave the farm. She'd grown to love it here. Summer was getting closer, and the trees were almost to full bloom. She loved walking there. It was magical.

"Lord, what are You doing? I don't want to confuse my daughter. I want to honor You in my relationships. Help me know Your will in this. Make it clear."

She needed to get back downstairs and finish making cookies with Erica. But she wasn't sure she could face Richard after running away like that. Her face flamed even now at the thought of facing him again. She was acting like a lovesick teenager. Sighing once more she decided the cookies could wait.

Closing her eyes, she continued to pray, seeking the peace of God to help calm her mind and her racing thoughts.

Twenty-Four

Richard

♥

Richard's encounter with Ryann had been impulsive, and he knew he shouldn't have kissed her in front of Erica. But when he'd entered the house after working in the orchard all day, a longing for family had overtaken him. He'd acted without thinking. Despite this, he had no regrets. He knew he should go after Ryann to apologize, but he wasn't sorry. Richard would kiss Ryann again in a heartbeat given the opportunity, and he fervently hoped another chance would present itself.

Now he stood at the bottom of the stairs debating with himself if he should go check on her or if he should let her figure it out on her own. Remembering his promise to never enter the second floor without permission had him turning away. Erica stood in the doorway to the kitchen watching him.

"You okay, kiddo?"

"Why were you kissing Mommy?" Erica stared at him with a solemn face that made her look older than her seven years.

"Because I like her." Richard went to sit on the couch and patted the seat beside him. The little girl joined him, hands clasped tightly together in her lap.

"Grownups are weird."

Richard held back the laughter that wanted to spill out. He didn't think Erica would appreciate it. He hoped his expression didn't betray his amusement. "Yeah, sometimes we are. I'm sorry if it upset you to see me kissing your mom."

He almost held his breath as he waited for Erica's response.

"It's okay. I don't mind when you kiss her. Jimmy Foster tried to kiss me at school a few days ago."

"Oh? Did you want him to?"

"No, I punched him." Erica shrugged her shoulders. "I don't understand why grownups like it so much. It's gross." She faked a barf into her hands.

Richard lost the battle. He laughed so hard he was in danger of falling off the couch.

"What's so funny?" The little girl looked at him with such a look of confusion as Richard worked to gain control.

"Always remember that. Boys are gross. Don't kiss them. Ever." Richard still had a grin on his face, but he'd finally gained some control.

"If kissing Mommy is gross, why did you do it then?"

"Well..." Richard scratched his head to buy himself a minute. "It wasn't gross. One day when you're all grown up, you won't mind a boy kissing you so much. You might even like it."

Erica gave him a skeptical look.

"What? Don't you believe me?" Richard chuckled as he ruffled the little girl's hair.

"Do you want to marry my mommy? Mommy said only people who are married should kiss."

Richard stopped chuckling as he stared at the girl. His mind whirled with the possibility. In fact, he was having a really hard time coming up with a reason why it would be a bad idea.

He took a deep breath. "Yeah, I think I do. What do you think?"

"I'd like that. I think you'd be a great daddy. Mommy was making cookies. Do you want to come help?"

Richard tried once again to keep up with the fast-shifting topics of conversation. He was getting better at it the more time he spent with Erica.

"That's probably not a good idea. I've never made cookies. Why don't you wait for your mom to come downstairs to help you?"

"Alright, but what should we do now?"

Slumping back against the couch, Richard let his head fall backwards with a sigh. The situation with Ryann had left him feeling unsure of what to do next. Turning to Erica, he suggested, "Why don't you go read for a while, honey?" He needed some time alone to think things through and devise a plan to fix the mess he'd created.

A small hand slid into his, and he turned his head to look at Erica. She'd scooted closer and was now cuddling against his side. "Can I stay here with you?"

Putting his arm around her, he pulled her closer. "Sure, kiddo."

They fell silent, and Richard started putting together a plan to win over Ryann once and for all. It was risky, but it was a chance he was willing to take. The stakes would be high, so he knew he had to do it right. He was going to need help. "Erica, do you want to help me surprise your mom?"

She sat up beside him, eagerness lighting her eyes. "Oh, yes!" she exclaimed as she clasped her hands under her chin. "What are we going to do?"

"I'm still working on the details, but it's a surprise. So, you can't tell anyone. Not a word. Not a hint. To anyone. Not your mom. Not anyone at the café. Not Jimmy Foster. No one." He mimed zipping his lips, locking them, and tossing away the key. "Not a single word. Can you do that?"

The little girl smiled and then did the same thing, zipping, locking, and tossing, just like Richard. She nodded her head up and down so hard she almost fell off the couch.

Richard shot out a hand to steady her. Laughing, he put his plan into motion. "Do you know your mom's favorite food?"

Richard stood in front of the mirror in the bathroom, adjusting his tie. He couldn't believe he was letting his heart rest in the hands of a seven-year-old girl who rarely kept her mouth closed. If Erica thought it, she said it.

But as of this morning, Ryann had given no hint she knew what was coming tonight. Except for one little giggle, Erica had kept her pinky promise to not tell Ryann what Richard planned for this evening.

His uncle's lawyer had called earlier to see how things were going. Richard had assured him the farm was coming along.

"When can I see some financial statements? You're already into the second quarter."

"Soon. I'll get them to you by the end of the week." Swallowing hard, he asked, even though he knew the answer. "And what happens if they don't meet with your approval?" He would hate to see the hard work he and Ryann had put into the farm go up in smoke, figuratively and literally.

"The fire department gets it unless you can show a profit. There's still time before a final decision. I want to see if you're on the right track."

Richard shook his head. He needed to focus on the now and not on what might or might not happen in six months. Standing back, he took a deep breath. Abigail would be here soon to pick up Erica. Then he would put the rest of the plan into motion. Once he talked Ryann into being in the same room with him alone.

She'd been avoiding him all week, using Erica as a buffer. Every time he had attempted to talk to her, she would make an excuse to go do something else. It was frustrating, but also kind of adorable. He'd almost cornered her in the laundry room one day, but thought better of it. He didn't want to make her mad at him. No, he wanted her to feel something else entirely.

"Abigail!" Richard heard Erica's voice echo down the hall. It was showtime. He made one last adjustment, nodded at his reflection, and headed out to intercept Ryann.

"But I don't understand. Why are you here, Abigail?"

"You'll have to ask that hunk of a man behind you. Got everything you need, kiddo?"

"Yup! Bye, Mommy!" Erica waved at the two adults standing on the porch.

"Wait! Abigail, what's going on? Erica, come back here right now!"

"It's my fault," Richard said.

Ryann whirled to look at him. "Why are you all dressed up? And you'd better start explaining fast because I'm not in the mood to have my daughter whisked off to Abigail's without my permission."

"Will you trust me?" Richard held out a hand.

Ryann placed both of hers on her hips. "Start talking."

Richard took a step back. "Okay then. I wanted to spend the evening with you. You've been avoiding me and using Erica to do it. So, I asked Abigail to take her for a few hours."

Ryann stared at him. "You did what?"

"Ryann, I've missed you. I've missed talking with you about the plans for the farm. I just wanted some time alone with you. Can we do that? Can we have dinner and just enjoy each other's company for a few hours without Miss Chatterbox within earshot?" He smiled, hoping she would agree and not demand to follow Abigail to take Erica back.

Ryann blew out a puff of air and let her arms fall. "I can't do this, Richard. I can't get serious about anyone right now. It's not fair to you, and it's not fair to Erica to have you in our lives and then have you leave once you sell this place."

He stepped forward. "Please. Trust me. I want to explain, and I will. Will you come with me so I can do just that?" He held out a hand once more, hoping she'd take it this time.

Sighing, Ryann eyed him once more. Finally, she reached out and took his hand. "Okay. But let me change out of this." She waved a hand at the faded, paint-stained jeans and Auburn Community College sweatshirt she had on. "It looks like this is a dress up affair. Give me ten minutes."

"Perfect." Richard watched as Ryann hurried up the stairs. Ten minutes would give him just enough time to grab what he needed from the kitchen and be ready to go. He prayed this evening would end the way he'd imagined.

Twenty-Five

Ryann & Richard

"W hat are you doing? This is crazy," Ryann whispered to herself in the mirror. Well, it might be crazier to be talking to herself like this. How could she have let Erica leave without double checking her bag or making sure she had snacks or doing any of the things she always did before letting her daughter be anywhere without her?

Ryann knew it was too late to change anything now. It would upset Erica if she went after her. She knew Abigail could handle it. After all, she'd helped Ryann out often enough over the last few weeks. She understood what to watch for and how to help Erica navigate her diet and blood sugar.

For once, she was going to put her trust in her friends. Her pulse gave a couple of quick beats at the thought. Blowing out a deep breath, she looked herself in the eye in the mirror and said, "You *can* do this. And you will."

And Richard. She'd realized from watching Erica over the last few weeks that she needed to live her life. Ryann prayed she was on the path God had for her, and she wasn't being foolish and letting her emotions rule.

She also needed to stop hiding in her bedroom and go downstairs to see what Richard wanted. He'd gone to a lot of effort for her. Something no one had ever done before. Not even Eric.

Over the last few weeks of working side by side with Richard, she realized how much she enjoyed his company. She looked forward to the days she could be on the farm. She realized she was happy. Happier than she'd been in a very long time.

"Here goes nothing," she mumbled under her breath before opening the door.

Slowly walking towards the stairs, she knew she was dawdling, but she couldn't make herself move faster. She didn't know what Richard had in mind, and something was holding her back. "Give me courage, Lord. It's time to live my life. Help me make the right choices tonight. No matter what happens."

Ryann gave a short laugh under her breath at her foolishness. If anyone heard her, they would think she was going into battle. Maybe she was. A battle for her heart, and she still wasn't sure what she wanted the outcome to be.

As she hit the last step, she heard a throat clearing and lifted her head. Richard was standing across the room, clearly waiting for her.

"You look…" he stopped and cleared his throat again. "You look beautiful." His voice came out sounding rough and made the butterflies in Ryann's stomach take flight.

She felt her face coloring at his intense gaze. She managed to squeeze out a quiet, "Thank you." As she started toward him, she told herself to stop acting weird. This was Richard. Little

Ricky. Her longtime friend. Even as the thought entered her mind, she knew he was more than that to her now.

And in that moment, her toe caught the edge of the throw rug near the door. She stumbled forward. Richard's powerful arms caught her, steadying her on her feet.

"Are you okay?" Richard held on as Ryann stood.

"Yeah. I'm just a klutz." Her face colored even more. She'd practically thrown herself into his arms. Ryann felt his grip tighten, and she looked up. Swallowing hard, the rest of her thoughts fled as Richard leaned down and brushed a soft kiss on her lips.

"Good. Now c'mon. I have something to show you." Smiling, he brushed his fingers down her arm until he found her hand. Weaving their fingers together, he gave a squeeze.

Ryann smiled as she followed him out the door. Twilight was here. The dim light was just enough to see the steps as they made their way down the porch.

As they walked past the vehicles in the yard, Richard didn't slow. That was odd. She thought they were going to Ellsworth or somewhere for dinner.

Ryann asked, "Where are we going?"

Richard gave her one of his heart stopping smiles as he said, "Trust me. It's not much further." He glanced at her feet. "Are you okay to keep walking in those, or should we go back for you to change?"

Ryann looked at her own feet. She had on a pair of sandals. "Depends on how much further we're going. If we're going for a hike, I might want to change and put on boots." She raised an eyebrow at him.

His laugh filled the night and Ryann joined along. She didn't know why he was laughing, but the joy in it was contagious. "No, we're not going for a hike. Just to the orchard."

He tugged her hand, and Ryann followed. As they came around the end of the barn, the apple orchard opened before them. Every tree was covered in white lights, softly glowing.

"Ohhhhh...." Ryann stopped, a hand going to her chest. "It's beautiful."

"There's more." Richard gently tugged on her hand, and they made their way down a row of trees.

After only a few feet, Richard stopped and turned. "This is the surprise." Stepping back, he swept an arm, presenting the scene before them.

A few years ago, someone had removed a few trees from the center of the orchard and never replaced them. This had created an open space which now housed a round table with two chairs. Two patio heaters sat nearby, their flames turned low. The table itself was covered in a white tablecloth and featured a large vase of red roses in the center. Each chair had a covered plate in front of it, and a bottle of sparkling apple cider with two long stem glasses sat on the table.

"Richard! This is beautiful!"

Raising her hand to his lips, Richard brushed a kiss across the back. Smiling at her, he said, "Let's eat before the food gets cold."

Ryann felt the butterflies in her stomach fluttering madly. She smiled as Richard escorted her to her seat. He pulled the chair out for her to sit. She worked to quell the thoughts that were trying to bubble up, telling her this was too good to be true. Her thoughts were not going to ruin this evening. Tomorrow would come soon enough, and Ryann could worry about it all then. In fact, she was pretty sure Jesus said just that somewhere in the bible. For now, she was going to enjoy it.

Richard leaned in from behind her and lifted the cover off the plate in front of Ryann with a flourish. She inhaled, taking in the delicious smells.

Clearing his throat, Richard straightened and intoned in a stuffy voice. "For tonight's entrée, we have grilled lobster tail in garlic butter with a side of crispy roasted fingerling potatoes and grilled asparagus in lemon zest. For drinks, we have water or sparkling apple cider. What would you prefer, madam?" He raised an eyebrow at her while he waited for her reply.

Wiping the smile off her face, Ryann answered in a formal tone of voice. "I will have the sparkling apple cider, good sir."

"Ahhh, good choice." Richard opened the bottle sitting on the table and poured some of the liquid into each glass.

Taking his seat, Richard then removed the cover from his own plate before asking, "May I pray?"

Ryann hid her surprise. She hadn't known Richard to ask before. "Of course."

He reached a hand across the table and took hers. "Lord, thank You for friends who help this bachelor impress a lovely woman." He squeezed her hand, and Ryann couldn't help the giggle that escaped. "Be with us tonight, as we enjoy each other's company. Help us see Your will in all we do. In Jesus's name, Amen."

"Amen."

There was something different about Richard tonight. And Ryann was sure her heart was in danger of being completely lost before the night was over. And a part of her was hoping for just that.

Richard wanted this night to last forever and yet he also couldn't wait for Ryann to finish her dessert. His nerves were about to do him in. She'd already taken off on him once before when things got a little too serious. And he was about to make them even more serious than ever before.

Ryann laid her fork on the table, wiped her mouth, and laid her napkin on her plate. "That was the most delicious thing I've eaten in months. Who made it?"

He held a hand to his chest, mouth open in mock surprise. "I'm wounded that you think I didn't make it!"

Richard smiled as Ryann's laughter filled the air. He couldn't wait to spend the rest of his life making her laugh, just like this.

"Considering you've practically begged me to do your cooking for you, it wasn't much of a stretch." She raised an eyebrow at him as she finished her glass of apple cider. "But did you make that?" She pointed to her glass. "Because that was delicious."

"Well, my uncle did. I found a few bottles put away in the cellar when I was down there last week. I've been saving them for a special occasion. This seemed to qualify."

"Oh?"

Richard swallowed. He hadn't meant to say anything yet. He needed to execute the next part of his plan first.

Pushing back his chair, he rose and moved towards Ryann as he said, "How about we go for a walk, and I'll explain how I whipped up those grilled lobster tails and the asparagus and..."

"If you can tell me the first step to making the asparagus, I'll believe you. Otherwise, spill!"

Richard laughed as he helped Ryann up from her chair. "Fine. I'm busted. Abigail helped. And her sisters as well. Even Erica helped a little with all this." He waved his hand to encompass the white lights hanging from the surrounding trees.

"How did you get her to keep that secret?" Ryann asked as she stood.

"With a lot of raised eyebrows and fingers across my lips for the last few days. Good thing it wasn't longer, or I don't think she could have done it." Chuckling, he held out his arm to Ryann. "Now, can I interest you in a short walk?"

"Of course." Her hand slipped under his elbow and Richard pulled her in close, placing his opposite hand over the one on his arm. This felt so right. This woman by his side again made him realize the life he'd been living down in Portland was a shadow of what he was meant to be.

Now for the last part of the plan.

They fell into step, and Richard led the way to the small overlook he'd discovered soon after arriving on the farm. The clearing gave a view of the ocean that had become his favorite. There was a large flat rock, giving a natural place to sit facing the water.

"Richard!" Ryann breathed out his name as they came up beside the bench. "This is beautiful! I never knew this was here."

"I think it was pretty overgrown when we were kids. I didn't remember it either. It's become my favorite spot on the farm. Would you like to sit?"

His heart rate increased as his nerves kicked in. Ryann gave a quick nod of her head. Richard placed a hand on either side of her waist and helped her hop up on the rock. He stepped forward, hands still on her waist. He wanted to kiss her, but there was more to be done first.

Twilight was falling, and he knew it would be dark soon. The light from the Haven Light blinked on and began pulsing as it made its rotation, keeping sailors safe even now.

Richard didn't sit beside Ryann, but sank to one knee in front of her, taking her hand in his. Her gasp made him hesitate, but only for a moment.

Richard's heart raced as he took a deep breath and began to speak. "Ryann, I never planned on falling in love when I came to Haven. I was just here to settle my uncle's affairs and sell Saltwater Orchard. But then, I saw you again. And I fell in love with you, and with the farm. I can't imagine living here without you and Erica by my side. So please, will you do me the honor of becoming my wife and marrying me?"

Richard held his breath as he waited for her to respond. *Lord, please let her say yes.*

Tears fell from Ryann's eyes as she reached out a hand to cup his cheek. "Richard, you've shown me what it means to be loved. And I know Erica adores you. Yes... yes, it would be an honor to be your wife."

Richard gave out a whoop as he jumped to his feet. He pulled Ryann into his arms. "You've made me the happiest man alive. I promise to love you both forever."

Richard pulled back enough to smile at Ryann, but he couldn't wait any longer. Threading his hands into her hair, he lowered his head to claim her lips. As their lips met, Richard knew he'd never spoken truer words. He wasn't sure it was possible to be any happier than he was at this moment.

Twenty-Six

Ryann & Richard

5 MONTHS LATER

Lifting shaking hands to her head, Ryann tried to twist her hair the way she wanted. Instead, the curl flopped into her eyes. "This is hopeless," she wailed. It was going to look like she'd just rolled out of bed. Why was her hair not cooperating today, of all days?

A gentle tap at the door had her hurrying towards it. Pulling it open, she spied Brenda and cried, "Help!" Grabbing Brenda's hand, Ryann pulled her inside and shut the door.

"Mommy can't get her hair the way she wants it," Erica said from the chair where she sat gently swinging her legs. "I'm getting a daddy today." It was all Erica could focus on for the last few weeks.

"I know, sweetie. You're one lucky little girl." Brenda smiled at her and turned back to Ryann. "Sit and let me see what I can do."

Ryann collapsed into a chair in front of one of the lighted mirrors. She couldn't believe her marriage would be the first at the new wedding venue. When she'd been planning the renovations with Richard all those months ago, she'd never imagined she'd be here today. Almost ready to walk down the aisle. But first, she needed to get her hair to behave.

"Are you excited?" Brenda picked up the curling iron Ryann had been trying to use, but she usually wore her hair in a high ponytail. Curling it was not something she did regularly, and it was showing.

"Me or Erica?" Ryann asked with a grin. "That girl hasn't talked of anything else since she found out."

"She has a right to be happy. She's never known the love of an earthly father. And I have an idea that Richard is going to love her well. And you too, sweetie. I'm so happy for you." Brenda leaned down for a quick hug. "Almost done."

Ryann watched as Brenda worked magic on her hair. In just a few moments, soft curls framed her face and the rest of her hair hung in waves down her back.

"There." With a quick spritz of hairspray, Brenda set all the items down. "Now stand up so I can really see you."

Rising to her feet, Ryann felt a little awkward under the attention. She didn't normally put this much effort into her looks, but today was special. She wanted to knock Richard off his feet, not literally, but if she could get him a little tongue-tied, she'd count it as a win.

"Where did you find such a perfect dress?" Brenda asked.

"Would you believe me if I said Marden's?" Ryann laughed. "They had a shipment from a bridal store the day before I went shopping, and I found this."

Ryann wore a simple cream-colored sheath dress that ended just below her knees. She hadn't wanted to wear white since this was her second marriage. Considering she found the dress at the Maine bargain outlet, it fit her style well.

The V-neck neckline showed off a blue sea glass necklace she'd picked up in a little store downtown earlier in the week. It was her something "new" and something "blue." While it was a little cooler now that fall was approaching, the long-sleeve chiffon lace jacket gave her the illusion of warmth at least.

"Mommy, you're beautiful!" Erica ran to give her a hug.

"So are you, princess."

Ryann had found a simple dress as well for her daughter at the same store. It had taken all her persuasion to make Erica leave it hanging in the closet until today. Her daughter had wanted to wear it everywhere as soon as they'd arrived home with it four weeks ago.

There was a light knock on the door. "Who is it?" Ryann called.

"Pastor Peter."

"Come in," Ryann said.

The pastor opened the door and stepped in. "You look beautiful, Ryann. Are you almost ready for the prayer moment Richard wanted?"

"I am. How are we going to do this, so we don't see each other? He's adamant he doesn't want to see me until I'm walking down the aisle toward him."

"We have it figured out. If you'll follow me?" Peter poked his head back out the door before opening it fully. "The coast is clear. This way."

Ryann had been surprised when Richard asked to have this moment added to the pre-ceremony part of the day. He wanted to pray with Ryann before they said their vows. Even now, a smile covered her face. This husband-to-be of hers was a definite keeper.

"Wait here, please, with your back right here at the corner. Erica, you stand on the other side of your mom so Richard can't see either of you, but he can reach your mom's hand. Okay?"

The little girl nodded and did as she was told. Brenda had faded away when they'd left the changing room. Ryann wondered where she'd gone.

Ryann closed her eyes and prayed while she waited for Richard. God had blessed her abundantly over the last few months. Who would have thought that almost a year ago now, she'd been homeless and living out of her car hidden in this very barn?

Strong fingers slipped into hers and her heart rate bumped up.

"Hello, beautiful," Richard said from the other side of the wall.

"Please tell me you can't see me." Ryann's free hand took her daughter's, and she squeezed, while trying to hold back a giggle.

"Not a thing. Pastor Peter made sure of it. He blindfolded me." Richard laughed, and Ryann joined in.

Quieting, Richard's deep voice began to pray. Ryann closed her eyes and squeezed his hand. She was beyond blessed today. The Lord had been good to her.

Richard couldn't believe he'd been so wrong. When he'd proposed to Ryann, he'd thought it was the happiest day of his life. Nope. Today was far exceeding that.

He stood in front of the mirror and adjusted his bowtie. It wouldn't lay flat. He was glad he'd asked to pray with Ryann and Erica before the ceremony, but now he was even more eager to begin.

There was a light tap on the door.

"Come!"

Abigail's head poked around the door. "Need a hand?"

"I'd love one. Maybe two." He smiled as Abigail entered the room. Without her help, he wasn't sure he would be here today.

"Here. Let me."

"Abigail, thank you for all you did to get us here."

"That girl just needed a little push. The rest was up to you." She smiled up at him as she worked to get the bowtie flat. "There. You're all ready to go."

Richard turned to look in the mirror. The barn had turned out just as Ryann had envisioned. Drew had worked twice as hard to get it done so it would be ready for them today.

The transformation of the stalls into changing rooms, lounge areas, and bathrooms was complete. The prep kitchen was perfect. And it was only right that the Three Cats Café was catering the event.

Ryann would continue working part time at the café, but her new position would be event coordinator here at Saltwater Orchard. Richard was excited to work next to her as they continued to grow the business.

He was meeting the estate lawyer as soon as he returned from his honeymoon. The farm was showing a profit. He hoped his uncle would be proud of what he'd done.

"Your uncle would love what you've done here at the farm."

Richard's eyes flew to Abigail's. "Are you a mind reader? How did you know I was thinking about him?"

"I expect the location had a lot to do with that. He would be proud of you, Richard. I'm sure of it."

He felt himself choke up at the thought. Making his uncle proud meant a lot to him, and Richard was excited to see where he could take the farm. Especially now that Ryann would be helping him.

"It's almost time. I think you'd better get yourself out there."

"Right. Time. It's time. Right."

Abigail laughed. "Maybe you should take a minute to be sure you can think clearly. Although, it won't last. The moment you see Ryann walking towards you, I'm going to wager you won't be able to remember your name, let alone hers."

And with that, Abigail laughed again as she walked out the door.

"Right. Pull it together Mosely. It's time to get this done!"

Taking a deep breath, he squared his shoulders and tossed up one last prayer. "Lord, make me a man worthy of her. Bless our marriage. Bless our life together."

Pulling the door open, he stepped out. He could hear the murmur of voices from just outside the back door. The fall day was perfect. Just warm enough that it was comfortable being outside, yet the crisp note of the approaching cooler weather was in the air.

They'd just finished the apple harvest. The first harvest since Richard had taken over the farm, and it had been amazing. The apple crop was abundant. They would have their first fall market the weekend after they returned from their honeymoon. There were already several vendors lined up, and Richard had high hopes it would be the start of something they could hold year-round.

But now was not the time to be thinking about business. He had much more important matters to attend to.

Stepping out the back door, the voices quieted as he made his way down the aisle towards the front. Pastor Peter was standing there waiting for him and smiling widely.

Richard and Ryann had forgone attendants. Erica would join them at the front, and that was all. They would become a family today, and he was eager to get started.

"Right on time," Peter murmured to him.

Turning, the pastor nodded to someone standing off to the side. Music filled the air. White lights were strung among the trees all around them, casting a glow over everything.

Richard had worked hard installing the sound system two days ago. It was the last piece of making this a venue where people would want to have their wedding.

"Here she comes," Peter spoke in his ear.

Richard's eyes lifted, and he saw Erica skipping down the aisle toward him.

"We're getting married today!" Erica yelled. "I'm getting a daddy!"

Laughter burst from Richard as his new daughter launched herself into his arms. "You're beautiful, little one!"

"Wait until you see Mommy. She looks like a princess!"

He kissed his daughter–he liked the sound of that–on the forehead before setting her on her feet beside him. Looking up, he was sure his heart stopped when he saw Ryann waiting to walk down the aisle.

Swallowing hard, he realized Abigail had been right once again. He couldn't have said what his name was if his life depended on it. But it didn't matter because he knew what was important. He was marrying this beautiful woman making her way towards him, they were becoming a family, and he knew he was home.

Also By

Other titles by Evelyn Grace
Seascapes (Haven book 1)
Sand Dollars (Haven book 2)
Seaside Chapel (Haven book 3)
Seashore Dreams (Haven book 4)

I love connecting with readers. Feel free to drop me a line at
evelyngrace@evelyngracebooks.com.
Follow me on Facebook: www.facebook.com/evelyngraceboo
ks
Check out my website for more information and to join my
newsletter: www.evelyngracebooks.com/

Acknowledgments

Writing takes a team effort. And thankfully, I have a great team around me. I want to thank all of those who have encouraged me along this author journey. In particular, I would like to thank my hubby for reading yet another romance novel. Some day I will have to share his editing comments. They are hilarious... "No self-respecting man would ever say/do that!" Thanks, babe!

I also wanted to thank my beta readers who give me invaluable feedback. It all made the story that much better. And I hope you all read it again because I lot was changed/added to along the way.

Thanks to:

- Emma Mancine, who always gives me a full on book report. I love it!

- Elizabeth Hatch, the best sister a girl could ask for!

- Molly Sparling, thanks for being a wonderful friend!